Mrs. Burton Harrison

The Carcellini Emerald

With other tales

Mrs. Burton Harrison

The Carcellini Emerald
With other tales

ISBN/EAN: 9783337027230

Printed in Europe, USA, Canada, Australia, Japan

Cover: Foto ©Andreas Hilbeck / pixelio.de

More available books at **www.hansebooks.com**

The
Carcellini Emerald

With Other Tales

BY

MRS. BURTON HARRISON

HERBERT S. STONE AND COMPANY
CHICAGO AND NEW YORK
MDCCCXCIX

THE PUBLISHERS ACKNOWLEDGE THE COURTESY OF
THE CURTIS PUBLISHING COMPANY (THE SATURDAY
EVENING POST), MAST, CROWELL AND KIRKPATRICK
(THE WOMAN'S HOME COMPANION), AND HARPER AND
BROTHERS, IN ALLOWING THE USE OF ILLUSTRATIONS

CONTENTS

THE CARCELLINI EMERALD

THE CARCELLINI EMERALD

I

How did Ashton Carmichael come by his aristocratic and decidedly individual place as a dictator in New York's smart society? Nobody knew; nobody really cared. In his set it was sufficient for one sheep to jump, and all the rest would follow. He was as much a power as was Beau Brummell over modish London in the days of the Regency. Asked everywhere, deferred to with bated breath by new aspirants, he was seen only at the houses of authenticated fashion. In the clubs to which he belonged—and the list of them was long, following his name in the Social Register—some men affected to pooh-pooh his right to membership; but rarely was there a member of a committee on admissions found to vote against him on the score of fitness. Good-looking, gentlemanlike, amusing when it suited him to be so, sarcastic—and, on occasion, offensively snobbish—his uncertainties of mood lent zest to pursuit by his admirers. He had no known income beyond that derived from a nebulous business in real estate in which he was alleged to hold a partnership. His place of residence was in a couple of cheapish rooms in an out-of-the-way neighborhood. But all the good things of life seemed to fall easily to his share; and winter and summer, on land, at sea, he was heard of, in ripe enjoyment of luxuries earned or inherited by other people.

As a matter of fact, while the general public languished in ignorance of Carmichael's antecedents, there were two or three individuals in New York who could have told his story from A to Z, but preferred for various reasons to keep their mouths shut. One of these was Tom Oliver, Carmichael's chum at college and his sponsor in the initiatory steps of worldly progress. Another was Tom's sister Eunice, now pretty Mrs. Arden Farnsworth, who, in days of lang syne, had been engaged to her brother's handsome friend.

The third was a brave, hard-working young woman journalist on the staff of a great city newspaper; a girl who never troubled Carmichael with her presence, although she bore his name, and had given all her little patrimony to help her only brother through the university and provide him a start in life.

4

It was at the beginning of senior year, when Tom Oliver came back to college to surprise his friends by the announcement of his rich father's insolvency. Up to that time Tom had been regarded as a prince of generosity and good-fellowship. His liberal allowance was lavished upon college subscriptions and other fellows' debts as soon as it came into his hands. Before the end of the month he was as impecunious as the rest of them. The blow of his sudden change of prospects did not, therefore, afflict him as much as might have been expected. As for the democratic, happy-go-lucky band who for three years had made him their hero, it seemed, if anything, to bring him nearer to their level. As a rule, the chaps of their brotherhood were the sons of toilers, accustomed to scant means and modest ways of life, who looked forward to opening the world's oyster with their own swords, or nobody's. The man who appeared most to feel the hero's altered circumstances was his room-mate, known as Ash Carmichael, a fellow the crowd had taken in among them through a not unnatural delusion that his being so intimate with Tom made him of Tom's sort. Oliver and he had drifted together in freshman year, and Ash was indebted to Tom for a long list of solid benefits bestowed with the same recklessness of

5

consequences and loyalty of affection that had marked every kind action of the young man's life.

On all occasions when it was possible Tom had taken Ashton home to New York with him for the holidays and flying visits. The latter had spent two months of the summer preceding senior year at the Olivers' house at Newport, where he had made acquaintance with some of the people who were afterward to be his sponsors in fashionable life. The stress he laid upon these individuals, their homes and habits, had elicited from his chum a great deal of good-natured fun at Carmichael's expense. But as that was the only thing he ever enjoyed at the expense of that individual, Tom was entitled to make the most of it.

For Tom himself the smart people who forever dined and drove and yachted and gave incessant dinners had no attraction. Mrs. Oliver, a devotee of the gay world, and Charlotte, her older daughter, who followed in the mother's footsteps, had ceased chiding their recreant brother, and were rather inclined to hustle him out of the observation of their all-important circle. Eunice, the younger girl, who adored Tom, used often to fall behind in the fashionable procession for the pleasure of sharing her brother's pastimes. In athletics Tom had trained her well, and here Ash Carmichael had first elicited her girlish admiration, for he was an adept in all sports requiring grace and activity.

But then even Mrs. Oliver told her son that his chum was the only "possible" college-mate he had ever brought under the patrimonial roof-tree!

When the crash of Tom's prospects came as to finances Carmichael was disagreeably taken by surprise. The manifestation to his friend of the exact condition of his feelings on this subject was, on the whole, more trying to Tom than the original blow.

The first public move in the disintegration of their friendship was Tom's withdrawal from the expensive rooms they had occupied together since freshman year into much cheaper lodgings.

Ash promptly installed in his place a wealthy and inane classmate whom the "crowd" had antecedently styled "Miss Willie." There was a groan of derision among the fellows for this substitute for Tom; and at an impromptu meeting of leading spirits in Tom's new rooms, in an old and shabby quarter, it was voted to give Carmichael henceforth what they called the "icy nod."

After the Christmas holidays, which Ash spent

with "Miss Willie's" family, something occurred
to bring upon Tom's former chum a ban more
serious than what had preceded it. The offense,
the discovery of it, the discussion, and the verdict were known to only a few of Tom Oliver's
most devoted henchmen. Outsiders, aware of
some dark mystery in process of solution, talked
of it—speculated curiously—but got no farther.
That Carmichael had done something awfully
shady was generally believed. What that something was nobody could find out. But during
the whole time of the agitation Tom went about
black as a thunder-cloud and silent as the grave.

If the Faculty knew anything of these proceedings it was based upon vague rumor only, or
came by intuition. They had nothing to take
hold of, on which to condemn Carmichael. It
was generally believed, among them and the
undergraduates, that a few men under Oliver's
leadership had rectified whatever wrong was
done; had saved Carmichael from disgrace and
exposure; and had then agreed to hush the matter up.

Before graduating, Carmichael took a prize
for an uncommonly clever essay, which he delivered with ease and distinction before an audience
of whom the strangers applauded him to the
echo. When he took his degree, and the class

8

was about to scatter, he was so much alone that nobody thought of asking what he meant to do in the future. When next heard from by his late associates Mr. Carmichael had set out on a journey to Europe to end in the circuit of the globe, as the companion of "Miss Willie," whose family defrayed all expenses.

About this time Tom Oliver, in a suit of greasy overalls, was beginning his labors in the repair-shops of a great railway in a little Pennsylvania town, to obtain intimate personal knowledge of all parts of the mighty motor that was henceforward to control his destiny. For, at the advice of a friend of his father, he had determined to work up from the bottom of the railroad business to as near the top as ambition and energy might ultimately carry him. Tom had need of all his pluck during the summer of this first apprenticeship to toil. His father, overworried and outworn, was stricken with apoplexy in New York, and suddenly passed away. Simply because he could not tell what better to do for them, Tom transferred his mother and sisters to live in a cottage in the suburbs of the town where he was employed.

Oh, the tragedy of life when small souls meet larger ones in everyday friction! Mrs. Oliver and Charlotte, banded against Tom and Eunice, made those summer days in the hot little house twice their ordinary length. And Tom saw, in spite of her persistent effort to make the best of things, that little Eunice was carrying a burden more heavy for her shoulders than the loss of a great house, a troop of friends, servants, and finery. Nor was it her mourning for the father she had loved tenderly that oppressed her. Of him she and Tom talked together frequently, and with honest feeling. But there was something else— something she hugged to her heart in silence, that grew worse as the summer waned.

Just when matters were at their worst with the little household—when petty domestic trials beat like billows over poor Tom's head—when Eunice began to look like an image of hope deferred—a visitor arrived. Tom heartily welcomed Arden Farnsworth, a man much older than himself, who in years past had been often at their home. A dim idea that Farnsworth had come after Chatty penetrated the brother's head. It occurred to him that among his mother's abundant lamentations for lost joys she had mentioned the fact that last winter she had been almost sure Farnsworth would propose for Chatty, but that he had gone abroad and made no sign. And Farnsworth, as everybody knew, would be a husband in a hundred—well born, well placed, of such character, means, and position as would anchor the whole Oliver family away from the quick-sands of their present uncertainties.

Then it came out it was Eunice, not Charlotte, whom Farnsworth wanted for a wife — whom he had loved for a year past, and left because he feared she would laugh at the disparity between their ages—nineteen and thirty-five—whom he had now come back to America resolved to secure, if earnest pleading would avail.

But Eunice, urged to the front by her mother, who philosophically made up her mind that one, if not *the* one she had counted upon of her daughters, should recoup their lost fortune and position, disappointed all the family hopes. She told Arden Farnsworth that it was impossible for her to marry him, and sent him away pierced with sorrow at his failure. His generous nature longed for an opportunity to place the dainty little beauty back in the niche where she belonged. For her sake he was prepared to make any provision for Mrs. Oliver and Chatty, short of offering them the hospitality of his houses and yacht and other such covetable spots where the Farnsworth Penates were enshrined.

In the tempest that broke over Eunice after Farnsworth's departure, Tom learned his sister's secret. She came to him, trembling and tearful, nestled in his breast, and told him that for a year she had considered herself engaged to Ashton Carmichael.

"What!" shouted Tom, loosening his hold of her, his eyes darting angry lightning. "That ———! Why, Eunice, it is impossible! You cannot have met him since I broke with him last autumn a year ago."

"Oh, Tom! How dreadful you look! Of course I knew you were no longer friends. It was just after poor papa's troubles began when Ashton wrote to me that you had separated, and that pride would not allow him to correspond with me after what had taken place between you. Then once, during the Christmas holidays, I met him in the street, and we took a walk together, and he begged me to be true to him and all would come out right. But still we did not write, until—"

"Don't tell me he dared approach you after *February!*" exclaimed Tom, white to the lips with anger.

"Yes. He said there had been such a bad quarrel between you he feared it could not be made up; but he asked me to meet him in town—in a picture-gallery—and I did. Don't be angry, Tom. He wanted to let me off from our engagement; indeed he did; but I saw he was in great trouble, and so told him I would never give him up so long as my love was worth anything to him; that he needn't write—I should understand. After this he began coming down to town to walk with me, which took place several times—I couldn't refuse him that comfort, Tom."

"Comfort! He was laughing in his sleeve, the infernal scoundrel, that he was so outwitting me! And I at that very time was holding him up like a rock, to save him from utter ruin before the world! But go on; for Heaven's sake, tell me all!"

"That *is* all, Tom. He sent me a clipping about his essay, and I was proud. Then he came once again, in June, to tell me he was going to sail with Billy Innis around the world—and from that day to this I have never heard from him." Her head dropped forward forlornly upon her breast. Large tears flooded her blue eyes and streamed down her childish face. Tom's tender heart smote him for having so increased her grief.

"My dear," he said, gently, "I would give anything on earth if you had confided in me before. In my desire to shelter a false and contemptible fellow I have let you run into a trouble that makes my blood boil to think of it. Now listen,

13

Eunice, and believe I speak plain truth. Not only did Ash Carmichael throw me overboard the minute our father lost his money, but last February he was guilty of a transaction involving me that might have landed him in state's prison if I had not consented to hush it up. Judge, then, if he is likely to present himself before you again. No, Eunice, he will never come back. He was a coward, a cad, a sneak, to gratify himself at your expense in that way; and my heart aches for you, dear. But now that you know him as he is you will never care for him again. Think how much worse suffering was his sister's, to whom he wrote confessing all, when he was in abject fear that I'd expose him. He had the cunning to make her come East to beg for him. For, at the first sight of that brave, tortured girl I was disarmed of my thoughts of punishment for him. For her sake, not his, I and two or three other men he had involved in the affair resolved to let him go and never to speak of it. Except to you, now, the matter has not passed my lips. And you best know why I have broken our vow of secrecy."

Again Eunice hung her head. The crimson of deep shame deepened upon her face. For a time her voice was stifled by the sobs that shook her frame.

"Don't cry, little sister," Tom went on, distressfully. "You make me feel like an ogre or an executioner. But in this case there was no such thing as being merciful; I *had* to tell you to cure you, Eunice. Heaven knows the task was not to my taste. Some day, if the opportunity ever comes in your way, I should like you to say a kind word or do a kind act to that girl. She is a perfect heroine; and, if she did not fancy herself under such tremendous obligations to me already, I'd like to look Alice Carmichael up and try to help her."

"You are bigger and more generous than I am, Tom," cried Eunice, between gasps of pain. "As I feel now, I pray God never to let me look upon one of their blood again!"

Four or five years later saw Mr. Ashton Carmichael a conqueror in the lists of New York's smart society. Among all the portals that flew open at his magic touch there was one that remained obstinately closed. This was the very fine front door belonging to the new mansion up town in which Arden Farnsworth had, two years after her refusal to marry him, installed his bride, recently Miss Eunice Oliver.

For Eunice, expanding into rare beauty during her exile from the gay world, had come back to take her place as a power in its councils, with a new understanding of people and things. Her grave husband was valued for his truth and loyalty and virile force, immeasurably beyond what her earlier love had been for his youthful graces of exterior. With all her heart she loved and was grateful to Farnsworth for "waiting till she came to her senses," as she often laughingly told him. Long, long ago the sting of Carmichael's treatment had ceased to pain her. Her fancy for him, in truth, expired that day when poor, blundering Tom had revealed her lover's treachery.

With the marriage of Eunice the pressure of adverse circumstances had been lifted from the Olivers. A former admirer of Miss Chatty's, a Mr. Ringstead, first discouraged by her mamma because she did not want her daughter to remove to Philadelphia, had gallantly come forward and offered himself anew. Mrs. Oliver, clearing her throat, suavely remarked to Chatty that she had always considered Ringstead a most excellent young man. To which Chatty pertly replied that his excellence was secondary to the fact that he was going to take her out of that hole of a provincial town where Tom had buried them alive. Mrs. Oliver, after the second nuptials in her family, gave it out that she meant to divide her time between her two married daughters and "dear Tom," whenever he could be persuaded to settle in a decent place; and a short time after went abroad, to the relief of all concerned.

Tom, during most of these early years a bird of passage between different headquarters of the railway that had annexed his services, was rarely in New York. When occasionally he had fallen in with some of his old college-mates they had dined and talked together till well into next morning, and word was passed along the line of alumni of their year to this effect: "Tom is all there, every inch of him"; "The same glorious old fellow"; "True as steel"; "Deserves his luck in business"; and the like.

But except for these banquets of good-fellowship, Tom had almost dropped out of conventional society, until Eunice Farnsworth at last coaxed him to make her a little visit and take a peep into the world that he had eschewed. It would do him good, she urged, to see some of the pretty girls and lively matrons who would be present at, for instance, a dinner to be given by Mr. Farnsworth's cousin, Mrs. Ellison, in honor of her daughter's coming out. Mrs. Ellison, rather a foolish woman Eunice must admit, would be charmed to extend an invitation to him at their request. It was to be a large affair of thirty guests, and Eunice wanted people to see her big handsome brother. "For you are the pride of my heart, Tom; and I don't care who knows it," she added, so genuinely that Tom was brought into prompt submission to her will, and promised coöperation in her schemes.

"Young lady from the *Epoch* waiting to see you, sir," said the servant at Carmichael's lodgings, encountering him in the hallway of that domicile, as he let himself in by a pass-key late one afternoon after a round of calls.

Carmichael was the picture of self-satisfied complacency. In attire, in bearing, he knew himself to be above criticism by the well informed; and yet his vanity did not disdain the looks of heartfelt admiration cast upon him by the hand-maidens to whom his landlady paid small wages for the promiscuous service of her house.

"Another reporter!" he exclaimed, petulantly. "Did I not tell you never to let them wait for me?"

"She's in there, sir, not in your sittin'-room," went on the girl, pointing to the closed door of the boarding-house parlor. "She said it was *very* important, Mr. Carmichael."

Smiling at the awe-struck expression of the

domestic, whose class can never rid itself of respect for private individuals "wanted" by the press, he opened the door of a long, narrow apartment with abundant cheap draperies, spindle-work furniture, and artificial palms, to find himself confronted by an unwelcome apparition.

"You!" he said, in a tone from which all self-complacency had fled.

"Yes, I. I was assigned to you, and I had to come. Until now I have been fortunate in avoiding such a contingency."

"I did not know you were in New York," he stammered, to gain time.

"I got this appointment on the *Epoch* last season, through a friend. But I came here first in summer, when you were cruising on Mr. Compton's yacht. You see it is not difficult for me to keep account of your movements, you are such a great man now; and besides, the others tell me you are very good in giving them items about your plans."

Carmichael colored. He could not believe that the cool, satiric, self-reliant speaker was the orphaned sister who for years had made him the god of her idolatry.

"You are looking well," he said; "your profession seems to agree with you. I hope you have comfortable quarters. And if there is any-thing I can do for you now, perhaps you will tell me as soon as may be, since I am engaged for dinner and have some letters to write before dressing.''

''They sent me to ask you the correct date of the Bachelor's Ball, and any items about the affair you may wish to publish,'' she answered, fixing upon his evasive eyes a pair of clear, bright orbs.

''That is easily done,'' he replied, with an air of relief. ''Or stop; leave me your address, and I will send you the full data to-morrow after the committee meets.''

''Send it to me at the office, please. But now that our business is so satisfactorily disposed of there is another little matter about which I should like to speak to you in a more private place.''

''But I am pressed for time, I tell you!'' he exclaimed, uneasily.

''It is something in the nature of a warning,'' she said, with a mocking intonation. ''But just as you choose, of course.''

''Come to my sitting-room on the floor above, then,'' he responded, ungraciously, leading the way up the stairs.

The room into which he ushered her was a

curious combination of elemental homeliness and the little belongings of advanced luxury, which littered it from wall to wall. Alice Carmichael's quick eye did not fail to discern this discrepancy, which she set down at once to her brother's habitual unwillingness to enjoy anything that was not a gift from some one who could afford to pay the piper. But despite her calm bearing, her heart was torn at sight of him. A thousand recollections, tender and poignant, arose to overwhelm her. To Ashton's infinite relief, however, she continued to sit as unbending as marble upon the edge of the cane-bottomed chair he had offered her. He knew well enough that after the first drop into sentiment she would soon be herself again.

"I have always regarded it as a particular piece of good fortune," she began, presently, "that so far as I have followed your fashionable career fate has not brought you into contact with any of the Olivers. When Mrs. Farnsworth returned here to live it must have been a considerable embarrassment to you to know how to avoid meeting her. But that, I suppose, might have been left to her woman's tact to dispose of. I am quite sure that neither she nor any one of her family would ever voluntarily come to look you in the face."

Her victim winced, and she saw that he felt the sting implied.

"Just now, with the omniscience of my fraternity, I am in a position to know the list of guests expected at Mrs. Ellison's dinner for her débutante daughter to-night. Not only are Mr. and Mrs. Arden Farnsworth to be there, but Mr. Thomas Oliver himself, who is in town stopping with his sister for a few days."

"The devil he is!" cried Carmichael, much perturbed.

"You can hardly have expected to go on forever escaping the sword of Damocles. Though, as you know, you are perfectly safe from Mr. Oliver and the Farnsworths, too; indeed, I don't believe they would turn on their heels to look a second time if they saw you lying in the gutter. But I have a feeling for them—a feeling that I can't ask you to understand — which makes me wish to spare them the annoyance of your presence. It will be the first time in years that Mr. Oliver has appeared in the society of his old friends. He has had a life of work and care beyond his deserts. I should like to think that this one evening's enjoyment is not to be spoiled for him."

"I believe you are in love with that —— monolith!" said her brother, with an oath.

Miss Carmichael looked at him with undisturbed equanimity.

"What Mr. Oliver did for me in my hour of greatest need would entitle him to the best my heart could give. But you forget, I think, that this and other experiences have made of me a machine, not a woman. No need, however, to tell you what he did for me, or what I am. Will you stay away from the Ellisons' dinner, or will you not?"

"I shall go," said Carmichael, stubbornly. "I am to take in Miss Ellison, and to lead their cotillon afterward. I could not be guilty of such a departure from good form as to throw over the Ellisons because this assorted lot of paragons of yours are going to be there. Among thirty people it is hardly likely I shall run counter to them. And should I do so, I fancy my position is assured beyond any attempt at a slight *they* could put upon me. My dear girl, your attitude in all this is in the last degree strained and goody-goody. Leave me to paddle my own canoe, as I have left you. We shall continue to do without each other, I do not doubt. No man alive could endure to have a Lady Macbeth kind of female arise and stalk about him indulging in remorseful soliloquies about his past. I am sorry that the only visit you have done me the honor to make me should have been devoted to such a ridiculous and futile enterprise. And you will permit me to suggest once more that I am really very much afraid you are indulging in a schoolgirl passion for your hero, the doughty and horny-handed Tom.''

"Good evening," said the reporter, briskly. "You won't forget to send that stuff about 'The Bachelor's' to me not later than to-morrow?''

She was up and off before he could intercept her. The little servant-maid in the pink cotton frock, with cap askew, was hovering outside his door as Miss Carmichael went out of it.

"Ain't he beautiful?" she said, with frank pride. "I s'pose you'll put another one o' them pieces a-praisin' him into your paper? There's lots of the newspaper folks come here to see him; and no wonder—an' him keepin' company with all the high 'ristocrats o' the city."

A moment more and Alice was upon the street mingling with the throng of workers like herself. Although well in check about matters of mere sentiment, for which there was no longer time in her hurried existence, her thoughts had filled with a vision of two children at their mother's knee, who shared everything in common until time and the mother's death and subsequent hard circumstances had forced them apart forever. Ah, well! she did not begrudge Ashton anything she had done for him. But she was glad their mother had not lived.

"It was so good of you to come early," murmured Carmichael's hostess to him, when her
guests for the dinner were beginning to drop in.
"Now that you are here I feel a great weight off
my mind. This kind of thing is rather a tax
when there is no man at the head of the house,
don't you think so? Please manage to slip off
and look into the dining-room to see if the lights
and ventilation are all right. I arranged the
cards myself, so I know that is as it should be.
You take in Gertrude, and on your other side I
have put the very prettiest young matron of my
acquaintance—Mrs. Arden Farnsworth, who
married my cousin, don't you know? I knew
your fastidious taste would be pleased by her,
and it would be a sort of reward for your leading
our cotillon afterward. Here comes another
raft of people. Do look at the table, won't you,
and tell my butler if you want any changes
made?"

Carmichael was accustomed to be deputy sovereign in many fine houses. But he had never
felt as grateful for the privilege as now. His

plan was executed quickly. So eager was he to effect a transfer of the cards of Eunice and her companion away over to the other side of the broad oval of damask bedecked with pallid orchids in silver vases, silver flagons, and platters of hothouse grapes, he did not think to notice for whom was reserved the place next Miss Ellison, whom he was to take in.

"What an escape!" he murmured inwardly, when Mrs. Farnsworth's cards were safely exchanged for two others, taken at hazard from the opposite side. "Our good hostess will think it was her own carelessness, but I am safe. I wish I had dared face the music, and sit next to my late betrothed. There isn't a woman of the year that compares with her, and I'd like to force her to notice me again. However, all comes to him who knows how to wait, and Eunice may once again be made to thrill at my words of —"

He started guiltily; but it was only Mrs. Ellison's sleek butler asking at his elbow if all was to the dictator's fancy.

"Very good, Masters, though I see you have taken on a little red-headed cub of a waiter who spilled champagne down my neck at the last Assembly supper. If I were you I wouldn't have the little brute at any price."

"Beg pardon, Mr. Carmichael, the man shall not be engaged here again," said Masters, in deep humility. And Ashton, having partially settled his score with a poor menial who had had the temerity to smile when he was laying down the law about the terrapin at a subscription ball, returned to the drawing-room.

It was quite filled up now with guests who had come in—the women complacent in gorgeous gowns, the men lagging, beginning to be bored, eager for food, and inclined to take pessimistic views of life by and large. They were waiting for some one, it appeared; and presently, as the door was thrown open, "Mr. and Mrs. Farnsworth and Mr. Oliver" were heralded.

Eunice, hurrying forward to explain to the hostess that one of their horses had slipped and fallen upon the asphalt, was royal in her young beauty. In her robes of shimmering rose color, her head, neck, and bodice coruscating with jewels, she stirred Carmichael's selfish heart as nothing in woman's shape had done before. He had to turn away to avoid showing his emotion.

"Don't stare after Mrs. Farnsworth and forget you've got to take me in," said, in his ear, the piqued voice of Miss Gertrude Ellison. "I declare, she has just bewitched all the men. I wish mamma hadn't thought it necessary to

put her next to you.   At this rate I shan't get
the least notice taken of me.   Luckily, I've got
on my other hand her brother, Tom Oliver, who
is as much a beauty as she is, in his way.''

Carmichael could not repress a movement of
tremor.   At that moment he saw going in ahead
of them Oliver, who had been his dearest friend,
his most loyal benefactor, whom he had betrayed.   And for an hour and a half he was to
sit so near him that their glances could not fail
to meet.   He wished now he had taken the
advice of his sister, and stayed at home.

"Dear me!" exclaimed little Miss Ellison,
coming to a halt behind their places.   "It's Mrs.
Dick Anstey who's next to you, after all.   I suppose mamma changed her mind about Mrs.
Farnsworth.''

"I suppose so,'' said Carmichael, stooping
mechanically to tuck in a corner of Mrs. Anstey's
apple-green velvet skirt, as that lady took her
chair, having permitted a servant to advance it
toward her and the table.   "That gown of yours
should be treasured, Mrs. Anstey," he added.
"It is the most charming you have worn this season, and that is saying much.''

Mrs. Anstey, who lived to dress, fluttered with
excitement at this compliment.   It was unlooked
for from Carmichael, who, until now, had snubbed

her unmercifully wherever they had met. He followed it up by devoting himself to her so exclusively that three courses of the dinner had passed before he gave heed to the heroine of the feast.

"You *are* civil," said Gertrude, finally. "I don't care, though; I have been well taken care of. Do you know Mr. Carmichael, Mr. Oliver?" she went on, with a coquettish glance back at her right-hand neighbor, to include the two.

"I know Mr. Carmichael," was the answer. Full upon his false friend's countenance flashed Tom's gaze of scorn. Little Miss Ellison, whose attention was distracted by some one opposite, did not observe this by-play. Carmichael was enraged at himself for dropping his eyes upon his plate. When he gained courage to lift them, Tom had entered into close conversation with Miss Cowper, who for some moments had been awaiting attention on his other side.

"What's the matter with you? You look quite pale and rattled," went on Miss Ellison, who had a talent for attack. "One would think you had seen a ghost. See, there is Mrs. Farnsworth looking this way, to make sure I am taking good care of her big brother, I suppose. Let us both nod to her and she'll know— Goodness! What *has* she got against you, Mr.

Carmichael? I never in all my days saw such a full-fledged specimen of the cut direct!''

Nor had Carmichael, in a much wider experience. His ears tingled, his heart beat with angry resentment. By not the quiver of an eyelash had Eunice betrayed emotion at sight of him, face to face. If he had been the footman, just then engaged in projecting a silver dish between her arm and her neighbor's, she could not more utterly have ignored his claim to her acquaintance.

"Evidently it's just as well Mrs. Farnsworth did not sit next to you," pursued Gertrude, at an age to look for little beyond externals. "I did not expect ever to see the great Mr. Carmichael come such a nasty cropper. She must be the only one of the 'crowned heads' who doesn't smile on you. But I must say she's the freshest and prettiest of the lot. When I get to be as old as *some* women I know, I'm going to stop playing kitten and settle down to be plain cat. Eunice Farnsworth's jewels are simply wonderful. Not as showy as some, but very fine. Mamma says our Cousin Arden has always had the most perfect taste in precious stones. The only time mamma ever got ahead of him in a purchase was in the Carcellini emerald, a relic from an old cardinal's sale, I think. It was

31

offered in Paris when papa and mamma were there—oh, long ago, when I was a little kid. Cousin Arden's order by cable, to buy it, came to the dealer just after papa had drawn a check in payment. Don't know the Carcellini emerald? Why, it's famous everywhere. The only thing approaching it in beauty and value belongs to one of the Russian Grand Duchesses. Mamma generally wears it at dinner, and I dare say she has it on now. If you have really never seen it, I'll ask her to send the ring down for us to look at.''

"Do you think she will trust us?'' asked Mrs. Anstey, who had turned to catch the latter part of Gertrude's chatter. "I have always been dying to have a good look at the Carcellini emerald.''

"Trust us? Of course. She often sends it around the table for her friends to handle. Now watch me telegraph her, and see if she doesn't understand.''

Leaning forward, the young lady managed to convey to her mother the request. Shaking her finger at the suppliant, yet amiably acquiescent, Mrs. Ellison drew from her left hand an object, which, amid flattering enthusiasm from her guests, began its journey around the table. Little cries of delight from the women, more restrained expressions of admiration from the men, followed the beautiful well of green fire in its progress.

"Now look!" said Mrs. Anstey, when it came to her. Slipping the ring upon her hand—a pretty hand, we may be sure—where it sent into prompt eclipse all the rest of her outfit of jewels, she held it up for Carmichael to view. "Did you ever see such a beauty?" she exclaimed. "I declare I shall go home and never sleep a wink to-night for coveting it! Such color, such luster, and such size! It ought to be on the turban of a Grand Mogul."

Carmichael said nothing, but he stirred uneasily upon his chair. The childish raptures of the speaker seemed to him like the crackling of thorns under the pot.

"There, Gertrude, take the tempter!" concluded Mrs. Anstey, plucking the ring from her hand and extending it with affected resignation.

"I tell mamma I will accept nothing less than this for my wedding present," answered Gertrude, receiving it in her outstretched palm. "But so far I can't get her to promise it to me. She says it must go by will to my eldest brother, a boy at school, who doesn't know the difference between an emerald and a bit of glass, the wretch! Look, Mr. Carmichael and Mr. Oliver;

33

I will show you something nobody else at the table has seen. The prettiest thing about the Carcellini is the way it answers to a shaft of light. It leaps up like a fountain and fairly bubbles radiance. See! I will lean over and hold it between my thumb and finger sidewise under this candle nearest us, and you can get the effect.''

As she did so Carmichael's eyes glittered and his breath came quick. A moment later a shiver of alarm and excitement ran around their quarter of the table. In inclining her head to catch the best light from the candle Gertrude Ellison had set fire to the fanciful aigrette of twisted tulle that soared high from her hair behind. The young men on either side of her sprang upon their feet. It was Oliver who, seizing the now blazing ornament, plucked it easily from the girl's mass of fluffy hair and crushed out the flames between his strong brown fingers.

''It is all over; I was not even singed, mamma, thanks to Mr. Oliver,'' called out Gertrude to her mother, who had just perceived the commotion. At once the inexorable law of conventional society closed upon the little incident. People resumed their interrupted chat, the servants circled the board as before, everybody had some anecdote to relate about a narrow escape from burning that had come under his experience.

And then, amid the murmur of voices, the tinkle of glasses, the strains from an orchestra that had begun to play a waltz upon the upper landing of the stairs, Gertrude Ellison turned upon Carmichael a perfectly blanched face.

"Don't give any sign," she whispered, "but tell me what I am to do. I have lost the Carcellini emerald."

Carmichael darted one swift glance toward Tom Oliver, like the tongue of a toad flashing out to catch a fly and withdrawing with its morsel.

"He knows nothing," she went on, petulantly. "He has been listening all this time to an interminable story Annie Cowper has been telling him. Who cares about her great-grandaunt's feathers catching fire from the chandelier at a Colonial ball? I suppose the ring slipped off down the satin of my skirt, and has rolled under the table. I can't make a fuss now, but I won't leave this spot while another person remains in the room after me."

"You are quite right to keep the thing quiet," he said, with consoling deliberation. "In a little while your mother will be leaving the table. You and I can hang back and intercept her after

35

every one has gone, unless you prefer to look first and tell her afterward."

"Oh, no; I dare not! I *must* tell her at once!"

"Very well, then; I will help you. If I stay behind while the other men go up to the smoking-room it will be thought I have matters to discuss with Mrs. Ellison about the cotillon."

As the company arose from table, catching the eye of Masters, the butler, he bade the men remain behind their chairs, and let no one approach the spot. He and Gertrude then hastened to intercept Mrs. Ellison at the end of the long procession, and make known to her the loss.

"I always told you, child, what would happen if you persisted in putting on a ring too large for you," she said, agitated, but (to do her justice) courageous in calamity. "In that flurry about the fire you must have let it slip to the floor, and being unused to wearing it you didn't at first notice its absence. Let this be a lesson to you, Gertrude, though I am sure you will find the ring, with Mr. Carmichael's kind aid. I will make excuses for you. People will understand your wanting to rearrange your hair. Mr. Carmichael, I trust everything to you; and I shall go on and receive the people who have already begun to come for the cotillon. Tell Masters to shut all the doors, and let not a soul cross the threshold of the dining-room until you give him leave."

There are heroines in all walks of life, and Mrs. Ellison, going forth to receive a set of gay people, consumed by gnawing anxiety to see the Carcellini emerald safely upon her finger, must be numbered high up among them.

"My dear Arden," she said later on, capturing her cousin as he appeared in the doorway, coming down from the smoking-room, "I am so thankful you have come. Your wife has gone home. She bade me tell you she did not feel equal to the cotillon, but that she wanted you to stop and help me out. Her brother took her home. How nice to see you, Mrs. Arbuthnot. Your daughters are looking charming; I hope they both have partners for the cotillon. Gertrude will be in directly. You know they are joking her about having set her aigrette afire at dinner, but it might have been something worse. Arden, I really can't endure this another minute. For goodness sake, go into the dining-room and see if Gertrude and Mr. Carmichael have found the Carcellini emerald!"

"The Carcellini emerald!" repeated Farnsworth, who, between vexation at his wife's unaccountable departure and stupefaction at his cousin's speech, did not know where to find himself. "Is it possible you intrusted it to Gertrude?"

"Their delay distracts me. If it had been underneath the table, at Gertrude's feet, where it might naturally have slipped down her satin skirt, they would have returned by now."

"What's Carmichael got to do with it?" asked Farnsworth, wrathfully. He, better than any other, appreciated the enormous loss of the splendid gem. "If I were you, Elizabeth, I would not intrust the duties of a host to a pretentious nobody like that fellow. Of course I'll go. I never heard of such a thing in all my life."

He found the dining-room shut, every door barricaded by Carmichael's orders. Servants and waiters were gathered curiously outside. At the sound of Farnsworth's voice demanding admittance, Gertrude threw open the door and ran to meet him, ghostly pale and trembling in every limb. Behind her, candles in hand, with which they had been going over the floor, already lighted in every part by the full power of electricity, stood Masters and Carmichael, both anxious and perturbed.

"Oh, Cousin Arden, I'm almost crazy!" cried the girl. "I can find no trace of it."

38

In broken words she narrated the circumstances of the ring's disappearance.

"I was kept in here during the search by no wish of mine, Mr. Farnsworth," said the butler, respectfully but firmly, when his young lady had ceased speaking. "It's a hard thing on a man that has to live on the character he gets in a place to be mixed up in an affair like this. And when you are convinced, as I am sir, that the ring is not to be found about this room, I should take it very kind of you if you'd go upstairs with me and make a search of my clothes without letting me out of your sight."

"Absurd, Masters," put in Carmichael, sharply. "Why, any one, to look at you, man, can see you're as much bothered as any one of us. He has been invaluable, Mr. Farnsworth; no one could have done more in our thorough search."

"You must excuse me for not inviting your opinion, sir," said Farnsworth, stiffly, confronting the last speaker. "I think the man is quite right in his request. Stay where you are, Masters, and when I have been over the ground here, and have satisfied myself the ring is missing, I will go with you to your room. Gertrude, my dear, do you, too, go upstairs and search every portion of your clothes. Don't call a maid; we need take nobody more than is necessary into our confidence. I'm inclined, as it is, to think the matter might better have been kept exclusively between the members of the family."

"I beg to be excused, Miss Ellison," said Carmichael, hotly. "Perhaps you will ask Mrs. Ellison to tell Mr. Farnsworth that I remained here at her particular request, to assist you in your search. The whole matter is abhorrent to me; but I think no gentleman could have refused to be of service to his hostess under the circumstances. And if Mr. Farnsworth has at any time any other remarks to make to me upon this subject I am quite at his disposition."

But Mr. Farnsworth had apparently no desire to hold further conversation of any kind with his cousin's guest. Gertrude, much overcome, thanked Carmichael, and ran away to her own room. There was nothing for Carmichael to do but to withdraw likewise; but he did not leave the house, remaining to perform his usual functions as a cotillon leader, with "distinguished success," as the newspapers said next day.

By the time the guests crowded again into the Ellison dining-room that night for a buffet supper, the strange tale of the loss of the famous ring was upon everybody's lips. How it leaked out no one knew. When Carmichael was consulted, he announced himself to be in the confidence of the family, and therefore preferred not to speak. No one felt like alluding to it before the hostess or her daughter, who were observed to "keep up" with conspicuous courage.

When the last carriage had driven away, the two ladies went with Mr. Farnsworth and a quiet, gentlemanlike-looking man in morning dress, who appeared from the regions of the men's dressing-rooms upstairs, into close council in Mrs. Ellison's boudoir.

"Try to remember," said Mr. Farnsworth, kindly, to Gertrude, who had begun to look drawn and haggard at the end of a lengthy discussion among the four, upon which finger of which hand you had put the ring when you began to show the emerald to those gentlemen."

"Why," said the girl, suddenly, "I had never put it on at all! I was holding it—so—between the thumb and forefinger of my right hand, turned sidewise to catch the light, when I felt the blazing up of my aigrette. Then Mr. Oliver jumped up and snatched the burning thing out of my hair, and scorched his own hand in doing it. It was all over very quickly. But I was so startled, I did not think of the ring for some minutes; and when I did, to my horror it was gone."

"Were there any servants behind or near you at the time, Miss Ellison?" said the quiet man in morning clothes.

"I think some of them may have run up to offer help, but I am not sure," said Gertrude, tears of nervous distress filling her eyes.

"But you *are* sure about the position of the ring as you leaned forward beneath the candle?" went on the same unemotional voice.

"Perfectly," said Gertrude, with emphasis. "In that I cannot be mistaken."

There was silence for a few moments in the little room with its pale brocades and Dresden figurines and gilded furniture. Then the quiet man spoke deliberately, drumming with a pencil upon the edge of Mrs. Ellison's dainty blotting-book.

"I have no sort of doubt, madam, that your emerald was stolen. Who took it, and who has it—whether we shall ever get it back—are questions to which I propose to devote my best abilities. If it was one of your own servants or employés from outside, the appearance and character of the jewel will soon put us on the track of it. But if—" He paused, and cleared his throat significantly.

"I had rather lose it," interrupted Mrs. Ellison, tearfully, "than suspect one of my guests."

"But you will surely not refuse to oblige me, madam," said the detective, with a deprecating smile, "with the name and address of the gentleman who sat on the left hand of the young lady at the time?"

This was too much for the overwrought mistress of the house, who broke down in a fit of hysterics that necessitated her prompt removal to bed and the summons of a doctor, who for some days kept her in the seclusion of her room, then sent her with her daughter out of town.

Although a nine-days' wonder in the conversations of society, the story of the Carcellini emerald had not, by a wonder, reached the public prints. The absolute refusal of Mrs. Ellison to proceed in the investigation, as far as her own friends were concerned, blocked effectually the roll of the wheels of justice in the direction of finding a possible thief. The other servants of her house, and the hired waiters present on the occasion, had, to all appearance, come out unscathed from the ordeal of suspicion, as well as had honest Masters. The whole affair seemed likely to remain among mysteries unsolved.

About a fortnight after the disappearance of the jewel, a newspaper not averse to the elaboration of savory personalities concerning the wealthy leisure class published a carefully veiled discussion of the affair at Mrs. Ellison's. No names were given, but hints were made of suspicion attached in a certain high quarter, involving a family of character and antecedents hitherto beyond reproach. There was a light touch suggesting that gallantry in the service of the fair may sometimes be made to reap rich reward. And the article, worded to excite curiosity without conveying facts, ended by forecasting a new chapter, at an early date, about the lost gem that would surpass in excitement anything so far derived from its adventures.

III

At this crisis of the matter of the Carcellini emerald Eunice Farnsworth, who had seen her lord depart for a banquet of public men, from which even her claims could not appropriately detain him, sat, one evening, quite alone. She had eaten a ridiculous little dinner of the kind affected by women deserted on like occasions, had retired to her morning-room upstairs, and was now sitting buried in the depths of an easy-chair, with an open letter upon her knee.

For the first time in her married life Eunice was unhappy. She had received that day, inclosed by her friend Mrs. Ellison, a copy of the mysterious newspaper article hinting darkly that the suspicions of those who knew were now turned upon a guest at the famous dinner where the jewel had disappeared. Read by a casual person the paragraphs were void of specific application; to the initiated there could be but one interpretation, and that connected with a most odious act Mrs. Farnsworth's own dear brother, Tom!

"I am still far too wretched and broken up to

think of coming back to town," said her correspondent, who wrote from a Southern health resort; "and Gertrude is just getting back her nerve and tone. But rather than let such an insinuation pass unchallenged we would do anything, make any exertion. Of course, there are only a few people who could understand the detestable suggestion; but the hint that more is to follow fills me with dismay. Why *can't* they let the whole affair alone? It is *my* loss, my misfortune. I have accepted it, and that ought to be the end. I have definitely withdrawn the case from the hands of the detectives, feeling assured that I could never take my place at the head of my own table again if I pushed the misery of suspicion into an innocent person's life—and that person my friend and chosen guest. Arden may say, and probably does, to you, 'Elizabeth was always obstinate.' Perhaps I am; but in this case I have already had more than my share of distress and annoyance from outside comment. They will be having it next that my own Gertrude took the wretched emerald. I wish my poor husband had never spent a fortune in buying it for me. But this much is certain: if it is necessary for me to come back to town in order to refute the abominable insinuation against your brother, I will do so—at any sacri-

46

fice. The only thing that occurs to me is that Arden may be able to choke off any further mention of the affair in the newspaper that has done us this injury."

"I could tell her," thought Eunice, bitterly, "that Arden has already been in treaty with the editor to that effect, and that he could get no satisfaction, the man declaring that if the 'gentleman' alluded to was guilty of the theft, his high place in society makes it a public duty to expose him, especially since the owner of the lost jewel has so weakly backed out of her responsibility to justice."

It was not a pleasant theme for thought. Eunice longed for the bright, strong presence of her brother to dissipate the clouds that seemed to close her in. But Tom was away in the West for an indefinite period. He had left town the morning after Mrs. Ellison's unlucky dinner, from which he and his sister had withdrawn simply because it was impossible for them, in self-respect, to remain for a dance of which Carmichael was the leader. Carmichael no doubt had recognized their motive in quitting the house. For this offense against his vanity, and the refusal to know him that had preceded it, was it possible that he—

Eunice sprang upon her feet. She had solved

47

the motive of the attack upon her brother. It was Carmichael they had to thank for the foul imputation. And upon this poor, lying, truckling creature, living upon his wits and the patronage of wealthy friends, she had once lavished the treasure of her young, impulsive love! A flood of shame and disgust ran over her. Then anger filled up the measure of her emotions. If she could only meet him—crush him with her disdain—make him confess the new offense he had committed against his former benefactor!

For Eunice, despite her marriage and the dignity that fact gave her, despite her husband's wise control, was still a very young, impulsive woman, and in that moment felt strong enough for any deed of righteous wrath.

A servant, coming noiselessly into the room, presented at her side a little tray containing a card.

"But I told you I am not receiving, Jasper," she said, without offering to take up the card.

"The gentleman said it is about a matter of business, madam, and that he will detain you a few moments only."

She glanced at the name, and felt a throb of the heart that almost choked her utterance, for it was the card of Ashton Carmichael!

Here, in her house! He had ventured to cross

her threshold! It must indeed be a matter of importance that had nerved him to come here!

"Say I shall be down at once, Jasper."

Her spirit rose as she went down the broad stairway of her husband's home. She was on her own ground, safely intrenched; he was the intruder whom a word could thrust from her door.

Something of this was apparent in her beautiful face, in her erect head, her eyes sparkling with indignation.

Carmichael, who had not sat down in the formal room of state into which they had ushered him, felt it, and winced. He had come there relying upon his unconquerable audacity, and to be so soon put at a disadvantage he resented bitterly. But he did not mean to let her speak first.

"I know what you would say," he began, with an assumption of humility. "I am a pretender, a man who pushes himself where he is not bidden; a villain, if you like. But I have some feeling left, and I mean to prove it to you."

She inclined her head with cold disdain, still standing before him.

"I put out of the question everything that relates to our own two selves—though if you knew all the story of that year—"

"You asked to see me on business, I understood," she interrupted, as if he had come to peddle his wares in her drawing-room.

Carmichael blushed crimson. The sting of her manner was intolerable.

"I came, if you will have it outright, to offer to save you and your brother Tom from the scandals that are already attacking his good name," he exclaimed, angrily. "For the sake of old times I can forgive your inhospitality, and even the insulting rudeness of your, and his, and your husband's manner to me at the Ellisons' dinner. I suppose you did not dream that entertainment was to terminate so unfortunately for you. The mischief this article in the —— has done him is, in point of fact, incredible. I happen to have some control over the situation—"

"Then it *is* your work! I thought so," she said, cutting him short. "May I ask why you presume to come to me?"

"You are determined to think the worst of me," he answered, growing white where he had been red. "I repeat that I came in friendship. I can be of service to you, and I offer to do my best. I can, in two words, get the forthcoming article suppressed, and will do so upon condition that you withdraw your enmity to me before the world; that you acknowledge and receive me in your house, and consent to overlook the past; that you induce your husband to treat me with common civility. This is not so much for me to ask from you—Eunice—the only woman I ever loved, who has gone from me forever."

For one moment her eyes met his, and she saw that he spoke the truth in what he had said last— that in all his poor, mean, warped life his feeling for her had been the best he had known. But even this feeling he would now make the vehicle of his selfish schemes. Eunice tried to compass, but could not, the infinite pettiness of the bargain he strove to make with her. Her brain, confused and shocked, refused to see, what came to her afterward, that he could not, at this crisis, afford to meet the open suspicion and hostility of a man of Arden Farnsworth's importance.

"I do not see—I cannot believe—that we should owe this to you," she replied, more softly. "I can speak certainly for Tom, that he would resent your interference in any affair of his. If I have done you injustice in supposing you are responsible for our annoyance, I am willing to ask your pardon. But I am sure— quite, quite sure—we can none of us ever believe in you again."

"You are indeed implacable," he muttered.

That she did not ask him to be seated cut him to the quick. He lingered uncertainly for a few moments, then bowing to her, took his leave. The footman, standing in the hall outside, opened the door for him, then was summoned back by Mrs. Farnsworth.

"You will remember, Jasper, and tell the others to remember, that I am never at home to Mr. Ashton Carmichael again."

The man, who, like the rest of his fraternity, knew all the figure-heads of polite society, went below and told his mates that there was "one house, anyhow, that cheeky young feller Carmichael was not to boss," and he was glad to see him made to eat a little humble pie. More than ever her servants admired their fair young mistress, whose wit and spirit and beauty, joined to her friendly consideration for their feelings, had elicited their unanimous and not-to-be-despised applause.

"You are very brave and sagacious, my little wife," said her husband, when she told him later on of her interview; "but you are playing an unequal game. That fellow, if my instinct is not at fault, will stop at nothing. And the key to the present overture to you, my dear, is that he's afraid of me!"

"What can you have done to him, Arden, dear, besides scowling most unbecomingly whenever he has been near?"

"I stand, in a way, behind Elizabeth Ellison, who, if she changes her mind—and women have been known to do so—and takes my advice, will run a very good chance of recovering the Carcellini emerald."

"Arden! What *do* you mean? It isn't possible you think—"

"Never mind what I think. Even to you, dearest, I am not prepared to say it in plain words. But this visit of his to-night, and his proposition to put us under obligation through this matter of Tom's, is the most impudent bluff I ever heard of. To-morrow I wire for Tom. He will reach here in the course of the week, probably; and we shall go together to that newspaper office and force a withdrawal of their threatened revelation. Depend on it, the matter of Mr. Ashton Carmichael will not rest upon this evening's work. The Carcellini emerald scandal is about to assume a new and interesting phase."

At the clubs that night, and in many homes next day, it seemed that people had, simultaneously and without apparent new provocation, adopted Mr. Farnsworth's view of the late excitement. Flaring up from the coals, the gossip about it began to burn with tenfold vigor. Some oracles went so far as to declare that Mrs. Ellison had recovered her jewel, had forgiven the thief (who had gone to reside on a ranch in New Mexico), and in token of gratitude for her signal mercy was about to present the Carcellini emerald to the Metropolitan Museum in Central Park. The hint given by the offending newspaper had not so far, prompted the general public to bring Tom Oliver's name into the affair. He was too little known to the makers of paragraphs and the purveyors of contemporaneous news items to tempt the fate adumbrated for him by Ashton Carmichael to his sister. But any number of wild, vague, irrelevant stories were started, and left to drift down the tide of idle talk.

When Oliver, much disgusted on arrival in New York by the revelations of his brother-in-law, was about to set forth with that gentleman upon the disagreeable mission of stirring up the erring newspaper office with a very long pole, Mr. Farnsworth, in leaving his front door, was intercepted by a visitor—a young woman, closely veiled, and wet by a driving rain, holding an open umbrella in her hand.

"Eh? Very sorry, but — private business, you say?—and I am not to speak for publication? My dear lady, if you could oblige me with the least idea of what you intend to say I could better—"

They were standing in the open door, Tom a little in the rear of Farnsworth. Both men were surprised at her sudden, impetuous gesture in throwing back her veil, and revealing a strong, excited face.

"Mr. Oliver! I must speak to you, too. Don't you remember Alice Carmichael?"

"This lady is entitled to the best respect any man has to give her, Farnsworth," said Tom, offering her his hand. "It is a long time since we have met, but I should have known you anywhere. Farnsworth, mayn't we step back into your little study, to the fire, and let Miss Carmichael tell us what is on her mind?"

"It seems that I am always doomed to come to you, Mr. Oliver, under stress of circumstance. This time, however, my errand shall be of the briefest. I meant only to give this"—and she held out a large brown envelope — "to Mr. Farnsworth for you. It contains, as you will find, the original of an article that was to go to press to-night. It was surrendered to me of his own free will by the author, who happens to consider himself under some obligations to me for past services. And it will not in any shape be duplicated or repeated. The greatest favor you can do me in return is to ask me no questions concerning it."

"Do you debar me from telling you that I am everlastingly obliged to you?" cried Oliver. "You can imagine what it was, Miss Carmichael, to be summoned back to New York by my good brother here, to find a mine of malice and filthy lies ready to explode under my feet. I can't tell you yet what the whole confounded business means. Indeed, I should be tempted to doubt the existence of this rot"—he gave the envelope a scornful shake—"unless you and Farnsworth vouched for it."

"If you don't mind I will look over the contents, to satisfy myself they are what we desired to get hold of," said Farnsworth, withdrawing with the parcel to his desk.

"Do, please," said Oliver, with a shrug. "I certainly shall not glance at them. Pray sit down by the fire, Miss Carmichael. I am sure your feet are wet, and you seem to be shivering. Let me ask my sister to come—"

"No, no!" she exclaimed, woefully, compressing her lips to keep back the tears evoked by his apparition. "This is a moment snatched from

56

business hours. I must be off. I am not cold;
it is nervousness, I suppose. Oh, think when
and how I saw you last, and you will not wonder!
And I have lately had much care. Please forgive
me, Mr. Oliver; I shall be all right soon."

Many and varied had been the experiences of
other people's griefs falling to Alice's lot in her
professional career. For so long she had been
in the habit of putting a lock upon her own feelings, while absorbing those of her studies for the
press, she could hardly believe she was giving
way to emotion on her own account.

She had spent the previous evening on duty in
the Tombs prison, gathering for publication the
last utterances of a wretched woman about to be
consigned for her crimes to life imprisonment.
From here she was going on to the tenement-
house district to write up the case of a starving
family for whom a newspaper fund was to be
created. Later that day she was due at a crush
reception, where there were dresses to describe.
Everywhere and every day of her busy, lonely
life, she was the human atom last to be considered.

"I suppose you think I am rather a lunatic,"
she went on, with an attempt at sprightliness,
seeing the deep concern in Oliver's face. "But
you must not mind my giving way to this weak-

57

ness. It is a relief to think that anybody cares. Now I shall go, please—not to keep you and Mr. Farnsworth longer.''

Farnsworth, a sheaf of typed sheets in his hand, came forward to join them upon the hearth-rug.

"This is the most diabolically ingenious effort of imagination I ever saw!'' he exclaimed, impulsively. "What would be a fair punishment for such a tissue of insinuations that can be read in two ways, yet would succeed effectually in damning the person they are aimed at, I cannot think.''

The young journalist crimsoned to the roots of her hair.

"I have not read it,'' she said, in a faltering tone. "I only—became aware—that it was in existence—and I was anxious to save it getting into print.''

"You have placed us under an obligation no money could discharge,'' went on Farnsworth, kindly; "but—er—it would give me genuine pleasure to express our gratitude in some substantial way.''

"No, no; do not speak of it!'' she cried. "Your wife will tell you, Mr. Farnsworth, if this gentleman does not, what a debt I am trying to repay.''

Before they could interpose she had left the room. Tom, overtaking her in the hall, urged upon her to accept his escort, or his assistance in some way; but with a melancholy smile she waved him off, and taking up her wet umbrella from the servant's hands went out alone into the rain.

"You don't mean to tell me that fine, frank womanly creature is the sneak's own sister?" enquired Farnsworth, when Tom, looking and feeling crestfallen, went back into the study to explain her identity. "It seems incredible! I think her shyness with us is because she knows Ashton inspired every word of this offending article, that she, by good luck, has been able to abstract from the writer's clutches. Probably some poor devil of a reporter she's come across and befriended. Jove! that girl was made for better things than a life like hers. I must set Eunice to work to get her out of it."

"You will not succeed," replied Tom. "She is fine and self-helpful and proud to a degree, as her brother is the reverse. There is only one scheme that suggests itself to me," he added, after a pause. "Somebody should marry her."

"It will be a very brave body who will saddle himself with such a brother-in-law," said Farnsworth, meaningly. "Don't let your chivalrous sentiment run away with you, my friend. Unless I am greatly mistaken, Ashton Carmichael has in his possession the Carcellini emerald, and will ultimately come to grief. What's more, I believe she thinks so, and that that accounts for her nervousness with us. If I knew more about him in the past I could better tell. I wish, in the interests of justice, Tom, you would answer me one question. Was the affair she alluded to of a nature to justify us in suspecting him of an act of criminal intent?"

"I cannot answer you," replied the young man, bluntly. "For years what I know of it has never passed my lips; and I shall never again tell that story."

IV

The morning's drizzle had settled into a steady downpour when, after concluding her notes upon the fashionable world as seen at Mrs. Hathaway's reception, Miss Carmichael, of the *Epoch*, put on her rubber overshoes, extinguished her smartest gown under a waterproof cloak, and unfurling her faithful umbrella, slipped down the steps and under the awning at the front door to take an east-side car for down town.

Her destination was not unfamiliar, for the car stopped at a crossing very near the house in which she previously visited her brother, Ashton. But as she rang the bell of his lodgings and awaited the coming of the maid, Alice's heart beat with fierce excitement. To do what she now purposed to accomplish would put into requisition her best courage, tact, and persistence.

She had written to her brother asking an interview with him at the moment when her suspicions first fell upon his complicity with the much-talked-of newspaper articles about the loss of the emerald at Mrs. Ellison's dinner. Upon his churlish refusal to receive her on any terms she had set her wits to trace out and discover the tool whom he had doubtless employed to do his noxious work.

This for a time she could not accomplish. But chance finally threw into her way the knowledge that on some previous occasion Carmichael had had so-called literary dealings with a man named Lance, a hack-writer of ability, whose bad habits were fast bringing his usefulness to an end. Now, indeed, fate played into her hands. The year before she had nursed Lance's child through an illness ending in the girl's death in her arms in the boarding-house where they were both living. For Alice, Lance would hazard his last hope of earthly happiness. She was to him a thing sacred and apart from his sordid world. When she sought him out, and asked him point-blank whether he had not been employed by her brother, Ashton Carmichael, to transmit certain information to a certain newspaper, the man was fairly staggered.

"Your brother!" he exclaimed. "That poor sycophant, whose pay even I blush to take? He whom we call among ourselves the 'Little Brother of the Rich.' Good Lord! You are as far asunder as the poles."

So Ashton thought, but with a difference!

When Lance understood the case he hastened with almost pathetic eagerness to bring his finished material and lay it in her hands.

"Is this little all I can do for you?" he asked.

"No, Mr. Lance. You might promise me never to put your hand to such vile stuff again," she said, looking him fearlessly in the face.

"The wording only is my own. He gave me the ideas. He said it would be a stinger to the man he hated most. As for the morality involved, I am past distinguishing between the grades of principle—since *she* left me, and I see no more of you!"

"There *is* something in which you might help me," she added, after revolving matters in her mind. "I need to see my brother—to talk with him alone. He has positively refused to receive me in his rooms. I cannot push my way there in the face of servants. Could you bring us together, do you think?"

Lance brightened.

"Why not? I have an appointment to wait for him at six on Friday. The people of the house are used to seeing me come and go, sometimes with a stenographer. I don't know if you are aware that he does a steady business contributing 'society personals' to our paper and to others. His terms are high, but they like to have him, because he's a sure thing. Will you prefer to go with me or to meet me there?''

"I shall be there at a quarter before six,'' Alice had said, drawing a long breath.

She found Lance sitting in the hall.

"This is the lady I told you was coming to take my place, Bridget,'' said Lance to the servant, pleasantly. Despite his shabby looks the maids of the boarding-house liked him, whom they called "Mr. Carmichael's clerk.'' The woman answered him in a jovial tone:

"All right, Mr. Lance. The young lady can go on up and sit in the sittin'-room.'' As Lance said good evening and went out she added, sociably: "You run right up, miss. Second story front. But, laws, I remember you was here before! Our Mr. Carmichael do be mightily run after by the newspaper folks. He's such a high-flyer in society. But he ain't well, I'm thinking; he looks like a sheet o' paper nowadays.''

The winter's day had closed in as Alice entered her brother's room, and sat down by the window, listening to the drip, drip of the rain upon the sills. She wanted time to think before he should come in.

He would resent her intrusion angrily, of course; but that would be nothing in comparison with his wrath when he should know for what she came.

For days she had carried fear around with her, and slept with it at night. Putting together one thing and another that had come to her about the unlucky dinner at Mrs. Ellison's, she had conceived the horrible suspicion that her brother was the thief of the ring. Since convicting him as the source of the slanderous article inculpating Tom, this suspicion had been growing into assurance. Until that morning her chief yearning desire had been to put Lance's article safely into Mr. Farnsworth's hands. That accomplished, she had for a moment breathed freer. Then the blacker weight had settled down again. A desperate resolve possessed her. She must recover the ring from Ashton, and restore it to its owner!

Did she not accomplish this, how could she answer to her dead mother, who with her last breath had prayed Alice to watch over the weakling of her fold, and to forgive him until seventy times seven?

Behind Alice was a line of Puritan ancestors who had lived and died strong in the faith and fear of a just God. Surely He would not permit her to fail now upon the threshold of such an endeavor. But how could she set about it?

How induce Ashton to confess his crime unless he were sure he was found out?

As the moments elapsed that were to bring the sound of his foot upon the stair the ticking of his costly traveling clock over the mantel beat louder and louder on her ear. Her brow and hands were bathed in sweat, yet she was clammy cold.

Six o'clock! He could not be long now.

Oh! she could never bring him to own the truth. At the first hint of her mission he would not hesitate to turn her with ignominy from the house—to brand her as an impudent interloper.

If the ring were here on the table before her she would even dare to take it, and escape, flying till she had laid it in the right hands, risking anything to save her brother from the consequences of his sin and crime.

A single jet of gas burned low under a shade of crimson silk above the writing-table, littered with fantastic trifles in gold and silver, spoils of his cotillons, gifts of his admirers. With fervid fingers she turned on the full light, drew down the window-shades and looked about her. There was no desk, casket, or piece of furniture that seemed a likely hiding place for so rare a treasure. He would never dare to carry it about his person. Nor, so long as the clamor concerning it lasted, would he venture to dispose of the Carcellini emerald!

Her face burning with another's shame, Alice went into the smaller hall-room, where his bed was and his dressing things were kept. Still the same commonplace furnishings, with a litter of clothes and boots and trinkets of the toilet. Here, too, she turned up the gas and lit it, terrified lest interruption should find her without excuse.

"For *her* sake," she repeated, to give herself courage in the search. Nothing was locked; all was at the mercy of the maid who arranged and dusted Ashton's rooms. With her old instinct of making his belongings tidy, as she had been used to do when they lived together, Alice began straightening the ties, laying the handkerchiefs in piles, and putting the gloves in pairs.

Forgetting her real intent, she smiled as of old to find behind a lot of other things a box filled with a hodgepodge of buttons, sleeve-links, cigar-cutters, scarf-pins, tangled with shoe-strings, rubber bands, and other flotsam of a crowded chest of drawers. This was Ashton all over, careless fellow! For the hundredth time his loving sister would extract the rubbish from things of value, and set the whole to rights.

Out of the confusion of this receptacle she

rolled a quaint curio in the shape of a thimble-
case made from a carved Indian nut, with silver
frame and settings tarnished for a long want of
cleaning. The trifle was too old and shabby
now to tempt anybody's cupidity, but it aroused
in Alice Carmichael a swelling tide of sentiment
that overflowed her eyes and softened her heart
to childlike tenderness. For it had been a gift
to their mother long ago; had lain in her work-
basket, and was once scrambled for by her children with eagerness proportioned to her withdrawal of it from their grasp. Later on it had
been given to Ashton, because he had first discovered the trick of opening it by pressing a
hidden spring. By some freak of chance it had
knocked about among his belongings ever since.

Alice took the poor little blackened relic in
her hand and went back with it into the sitting-
room, where she dropped upon a chair, abandon-
ing herself to retrospect. Away flew the
hideous nightmare of her present quest. Ashton
and she were children together, she loving him,
sheltering him, proud of his beauty and accomplishments, following his lead with blind idolatry.

With this amulet in her grasp she longed to
clasp him again in her arms, to talk with him of
their mother, their old home; to laugh and chaff
with him about the things of every day.

Mechanically her fingers fumbled with the thimble-case, turning it over and over to feel for the point of the carving that concealed its mystery. Smiling, she discovered at last the spring—touched it—the nut flew open—something dropped into her lap that she reached down to regain. She was astounded to find her fingers close upon a gem that at the gleam of gas-light falling full upon its lustrous surface sent up a bubbling, dazzling fount of greenish flame! She started with a convulsive movement of dismay. There could be no doubt that she held in her hand the Carcellini emerald!

Then flowed upon her soul a torrent of deepest misery. Once before her brother had been guilty of a theft—of moneys laid to Tom Oliver's account as treasurer of a college fund. But she had paid that out of her poor earnings, and Tom, for her sake, had offered to hush the matter up, and give Ashton "another chance."

And thus he had used his chance! The flaring radiance of the jewel seemed to taunt her anguish.

What should she do? Whither should she turn to save him once again? Rising, her feet refused to sustain her. As she stood dizzy, trembling, aghast, holding the precious jewel as she looked at it, the door opened and her brother came into the room. His eyes flashed anger at sight of her, but something more devilish inspired him when he saw what she had in her hand.

In two bounds he was across the room and had seized her. She shut her eyes, and uttered a prayer to God for strength. She was wiry and vigorous, and did not mean to let Ashton take the emerald from her if she could help it. At all costs she would save him from himself. He said not a word, nor did she. Each was fiercely determined to conquer in the struggle. Too well he knew that if he could regain his stolen prize, and turn her from his room, her lips would be sealed as before.

But he was not prepared for her physical resistance. At his approach she had slipped the gem into hiding in her dress, keeping her right hand clenched as if she still held it in her grasp.

Without mercy he bent her arm back and forth, hurting her cruelly, and at last, forcing her bruised fingers apart, saw that she held nothing between them. Then with a savage oath he struck her full across the face!

Alice staggered back, stunned and dismayed. But she did not waver in her intention to get by him to the door, and thence make her escape into the street. Once free of Ashton she would carry the jewel to Mr. Farnsworth or Tom Oliver if she could not reach its owner.

Ashton divined her scheme. His only hope lay in keeping her prisoner till he could force her to give up the gem. With more brutal words he started to cut off her retreat by putting his back against the door. His whole appearance was transformed by furious passion.

At that moment help came to her from a quarter on which she had not counted. She saw her brother shiver all over, and grow deadly pale. His left hand made a clutching movement toward his heart; he staggered forward, and fell—into her arms.

Alice had seen this once before—an occasion never to be forgotten. She knew the terror-stricken eyes, the awful, helpless appeal for relief from sudden oppression. His livid features brought back to her with agonizing force the face of their dying mother under like conditions. Exerting all her powers she dragged him to a sofa, laid him down, and flew to ring the bell, peal upon peal.

The maid who ran up to answer it gave one frightened glance into the room and rushed back to the landing to summon help from any one who might be passing on the stairs. Her call brought among others a gentleman just admitted into the hall below. In the maze of her feelings Alice hardly felt surprised to see Tom Oliver entering her brother's room. She begged him, pathetically, to explain to the proprietors of the house her right to be there, then went on her knees again beside the prostrate form upon the lounge. In a very few moments a physician came, and Alice, giving place to him, let Tom lead her over to a window, where he left her looking out into the night.

Returning presently he toıd her that all was over. Ashton had died without coming back to consciousness.

"You will let me take charge of everything," he added, with deep feeling in his voice. "When I stood with the doctor looking down at him I forgot what I came here to say—everything, in fact, but that I once loved him like a brother."

"I think I know what you came for," she answered, wistfully. "You meant to silence him for the future, and now death has done it— oh, how awfully!"

She shuddered. The pain of her body was beginning to make itself severely felt. It recalled to her the prize for which she had risked so much, that lay close to the tumultuous beatings of her heart. Above all things she longed for advice from Tom concerning it, but could not bring herself to speak the words that would incriminate the dead.

When, some months later Tom Olivei asked Alice Carmichael to be his wife she tried to make him understand that in addition to other reasons why she could not accept his "generous sacrifice," there was one supreme obstacle between them.

"Do not tell me," he said, with authority, "what you conceive this to be. I know all that I care to know of what has kept us apart till now. It is the future, not the past, that you and I have to deal with. I shall take you to live far away from the scenes of your sorrowful memories—and for the rest trust me!"

But no man, however thoughtful, however loving, can extinguish in a faithful woman's heart the flame of her earliest tenderness. Often and again Alice Oliver thinks of the lonely, unhonored grave in which lies one who is never mentioned in her little family. Less often—but now always kindly—Eunice Farnsworth thinks of him, too.

The restoration to its owner of the great Carcellini emerald—without the ring—is well known

73

to have occurred directly upon Mrs. Ellison's return to town from her Southern journey. It was sent back to her as mysteriously as it had vanished. No clew was ever found that informed the public of the author of either its disappearance or its reappearance.

AN AUTHOR'S READING AND
ITS CONSEQUENCES

.

AN AUTHOR'S READING AND ITS CONSEQUENCES

For some time Sutphen had been in proud possession of a Literary Club, the leading spirit of which organization was the lively and irrepressible wife of the chief banker of the town.

People in Sutphen, including her family, her followers and, last but not least, her husband, never knew what Mrs. Chauncey Stratton was going to do next for the benefit or entertainment of their lives. She rushed them from bazaar to out-door play, from concerts to cooking classes. She and her coterie of womenfolk had descended upon the editor of the principal newspaper, and made him give them one issue of his journal to be edited by them for charity. And about six months before she had instituted a series of fortnightly meetings, at which men and women were to meet for discussion of books and current events. After the president (of course, Mrs. Chauncey Stratton) had accomplished the matter of reading before the assembled club two or three papers embodying her own views of given subjects, and was getting a little tired of it, her friends began dimly to feel that something new would shortly be in order to brighten these occasions—something fresh and metropolitan, *fin de siècle*, that would carry Sutphen again up on the wave of novelty.

But like all great leaders, Mrs. Chauncey Stratton had malcontents in her camp—close to her person—sharing in her daily councils. The chief complaint made in vulgar parlance by these unsatisfied ones was that they were tired of being bossed.

The matter was under discussion one morning in the cozy library of the secretary of the club, a well-to-do spinster, Miss Cornelia Bennett, whose claim to literary cousinship was based upon substantial grounds. For some years she had been in the habit of sending slips of linen cloth to authors in America and Europe, with the request that they would inscribe thereon their names in pencil. These autographs, duly returned to and "backstitched" in color by Cornelia, were then assembled in a sort of "crazy quilt," and sold for the benefit of a hospital for incurables. After this signal success in the world of letters, Miss Bennett had been elected without a dissenting voice to be Mrs. Stratton's second in command. She was a meek, ashen-

hued female, who, to all appearance, accepted
it as her manifest destiny to walk in Mrs. Stratton's tracks, never dreaming of such defiance as
pushing ahead of her, or crossing her line of
march.   But, in reality, while engaged in covering for distribution among the members of the
club the batch of new books ordered by Mrs.
Stratton from New York, a strange spirit of
revolt was kindling in her flat chest.   Aiding
Miss Bennett in her work, sat Mrs. Mark Grindstone, a large, dull, catarrhal lady, chosen to
serve as treasurer of their organization—chiefly
because she lived in a large, dull house, was
sustained by a large, dull husband, and wore to
church on Sundays a black velvet cloak bursting
with jet beads and bugles at every pore.

Dull as Mrs. Grindstone was, she yet possessed the spirit of the traditional worm.   "Of
what use is it," she asked herself, "to wear the
handsomest cloak in Sutphen, if one is always to
be ordered to the right about by Annetta Stratton?"

And "Why have I been in correspondence with
the most prominent brain-workers of two hemi-
spheres," wondered Cornelia, "if here I am
actually afraid to portion out the books before
Annetta Stratton comes? If we had only a
chance!" she murmured, making common cause

with Mrs. Grindstone, "to show her that when called upon for independent action, we can be her equals in success."

"We will make a chance," said Mrs. Grindstone, after clearing her throat, rather unpleasantly, Cornelia thought. "What Annetta does not like to think is that other people can do things without her telling them how. It would be a good plan to keep quiet and go ahead, and do some big thing exactly as she means to do it—on the same scale, in every way."

"Exactly!" said Cornelia, with animation, as she wrestled with the crackly brown paper enshrouding the last book of her pile. "One such lesson would be enough for Annetta."

"Just so," said Mrs. Grindstone, fairly slapping her last label into place.

"Look here, girls," interposed old Mrs. Bennett, who always read her morning's paper from the rising to the going down of its varied information; "fine times have come to Sutphen. Here's a city caterer set up in that built-over block on Main Street, where Blink's shoe-store used to be before the fire. There's nothing he doesn't offer to furnish to customers—bread, rolls, patty shells, ice-creams (French and American), birthday cakes, weddin' cakes, salads, cotillon favors, Jack Horner pies—"

"AN OPPORTUNITY TO DECK OUT HER BOARD WITH AN EFFECT."

"You don't say so?" interpolated Mrs. Grindstone with housekeeperish relish.

"Yes; and he undertakes to serve 'dinners, luncheons, teas, and receptions with glass, silverware, and elegant services of china, competent waiters and chefs, awnings, camp-chairs, crash, tables, decorations—all in first-class style!'"

"For all the world as they do it in the city," exclaimed Miss Cornelia, excitedly. "Mother, it does look as if Providence had rolled a stone out of our pathway. Everybody knows we could have had just as fine parties as Annetta Stratton if we'd only not had to ask her how to set about givin' 'em. And so could you, Mrs. Grindstone. Your house is two feet wider than Annetta's, four rooms on a floor, and splendid chandeliers in every room. Just the place for an evening reception, like the one I went to at Professor Slocum's in New York."

"I have often thought of it," sighed Mrs. Grindstone. "Of course, there'd be some trouble to get Mr. Grindstone into it. He's sort o' set in his ways, and thinks it a sin to light more than one gas burner in a room. But we might get over *him*, if there was only any excuse to give a party—any brides or explorers or great folks that we knew, coming to town, that had to be entertained."

"That's it," said Miss Cornelia. "We are as dull as ditchwater in Sutphen—unless Annetta stirs us up," she added, reluctantly.

At this moment, enter Mrs. Chauncey Stratton, plump, rustling, well-dressed, with red cheeks like a china doll, self-satisfaction in every line of her face, in every movement of her person. At the bare sight of her the two conspirators shrunk into their shells. Old Mrs. Bennett, who had returned to the perusal of a column devoted to the wants of domestic service, alone preserved her equilibrium.

"My dear girls," exclaimed the oracle, dropping into her chair at the literary table, "if I am late, put it down to the claims of excessive correspondence. And as I see you've finished with the books, let me lose no time in informing you that I have just had the good fortune to conclude successfully a negotiation for a lecture before our club from no less a literary light than Timothy Bludgeon, who is at the —— Hotel in New York."

"Bludgeon, the English author!" replied Miss Cornelia, faintly. "Not that I've much opinion of his works, since he refused me his autograph for my quilt, and even sent me a very tart letter through his secretary. But, still, he is the lion of the day."

"Precisely," observed Mrs. Stratton calmly; "so I made up my mind to get him—and I did!"

Mrs. Grindstone made a series of muffled sounds that might have been applause. In her heart she was struck with jealous indignation. Quick as a flash she and Cornelia saw open before them another vista in which Annetta would walk glorified, they remaining part of the inconspicuous crowd ranged on either side of her.

"I asked him to come for our meeting on the fifteenth," remarked Mrs. Stratton, with the same exasperating composure born of certainty. "And he could just fit it in on his way to Boston. He will arrive on the 11 A.M. train on the fifteenth, and leave next morning at the same time, thus allowing to Sutphen just twenty-four hours. I have decided to give him a dinner in the evening, and to change the hour for the lecture to the afternoon."

"Such assurance!" said both satellites internally. But they only murmured, "Splendid!" "Just like you, Annetta," and the like.

"Of course, you and dear Mr. Grindstone will be included in my dinner list," went on Mrs. Stratton, addressing her now speechless treasurer. "And you, Cornelia, will pair with old Major Gooch. Sixteen I can seat easily, all choice spirits, and the rest of the club will have to be satisfied with an introduction to Bludgeon over a cup of tea at five o'clock. Mr. Bludgeon will, I fancy, see that Sutphen is not so far behind New York in her style of doing things."

"And what will the lecture be about?" ventured Cornelia, more than anything else to cover her own pique.

"Oh, that is of no consequence! Readings from his own works, possibly. But the name of Bludgeon is enough. It will exhaust a good deal of the reserve fund of the club to pay him his price, but I felt sure we could make that all right, Mrs. Grindstone. That I had decided it is best would, of course, be sufficient for the club."

And the treasurer was to have no voice in this, her own especial branch of service! No wonder Mrs. Grindstone's spirit rose! Old Mrs. Bennett, breaking in upon the conversation to read aloud an obituary notice striking her fancy, effected a happy diversion.

From that date Mrs. Stratton, absorbed in her own ambitious plans for a feast to the English author that should be described in the local prints, and perchance quoted in metropolitan news columns, saw but little of her two friends. It was observed by some lookers-on that Cornelia

Bennett was seen moving about the streets with animation, paying frequent visits to the new caterer, Simonson, and preserving withal an air of pleasing mystery. Other people saw good Mrs. Grindstone going hither and thither in much the same way. And putting two and two together, Sutphen decided that there was to be at least a "chicken salad and oyster spread" in store for the members of the Literary Club, following the appearance on their platform of the great man, Timothy Bludgeon. The unliterary portion of Sutphen licked its chops at the suggestion!

But a week before the appointed time, out came a genuine surprise. Two sets of cards were issued simultaneously. One from Mrs. and Miss Bennett, inviting their friends to meet Mr. Bludgeon at luncheon on the fifteenth; the other stating that Mr. and Mrs. Grindstone would be "At Home" on the evening of the same day, at half-past ten o'clock, with the additional words, "To meet Mr. Bludgeon" inscribed across the tops!

Where now was the wind to fill Mrs. Stratton's sails? In vain might she whistle for it, when her lion was due to roar at two banquets besides her own in the self-same day. And worse than all, Cornelia Bennett, in undertaking to give this ridiculous luncheon of hers, would actually take precedence in point of time of Mrs. Chauncey Stratton! Of course the affair would be a sad failure. Cornelia knew little, her mother less, of the customs of entertaining in modern society. Theirs would be homely doings. Turkey with cranberry sauce, for example; jellies in tall glasses set around a china *compotier* of floating island; cakes, big and little. No lobster *farcie*, no mushroom on toast, French chops, birds, tongue in aspic, salads, ices—such as Mrs. Stratton would have ordered. Mrs. Grindstone's festivity would be—equally, of course—on the same old-fashioned lines. Oyster stews and molds of ice-cream, the predominating element of the table. A smell of fried oysters enveloping all. Oh! Annetta well knew the sort of thing to expect. She pitied poor Mr. Bludgeon for falling into the hands of these stupid, pushing women, who were not satisfied to sit still and see her take the field of Sutphen's hospitality to distinguished strangers. One thought occurred to her, to fill Annetta's soul with consolation! The weak spot in Sutphen's domestic panoply, as known to all Sutphen's housekeepers, was the general prevalence of plain white or old willow-pattern china on the shelves. Most of Sutphen's lords and masters preferred these varieties of porcelain, and had set their feet down upon any suggestion of change. Strange to say, even the amenable Mr. Chauncey Stratton had once asserted himself so far as to declare he preferred to eat his meals from the dishes he had been accustomed to ever since his wife and he had set up housekeeping. This was the crumpled roseleaf in Mrs. Chauncey Stratton's couch of down. That her set of white porcelain rejoiced in gilded edges, while those of other people were plain, gave her but limited satisfaction. For two years she had been bending every energy of her mind toward securing a set of Royal Meissen—"onion pattern"—that she had seen in a famous shop in New York. For two years Mr. Chauncey Stratton had resisted her. His attitude was to be accounted for only by the saying of old Mrs. Bennett, "The very best and most biddable of husbands has his obstinate spot, my dear; and when a woman runs afoul of it, she might as well give up."

Of late, coincidently with the threatened dinner to Mr. Timothy Bludgeon, Mrs. Stratton had seen a ray of light pierce the darkness surrounding this question of china for the table. In investigating the resources of Simonson, the New York *restaurateur*, her eyes had sparkled at the discovery in the rear of his premises of an entire service of "onion pattern" Meissen—or at least a good imitation of that desired original.

What an opportunity was here to deck out her board with an "effect" in porcelain of the latter-day style she aspired to introduce into Sutphen.

Little by little, the wily caterer had induced her to trust the whole thing into his hands. In cases where Simonson undertook to serve the feast throughout, it was his custom, he said, to supply also the table service, china, silver, dishes, candelabra, rose-colored candles with shades to match, side-dishes for bonbons—all. Under these conditions he guaranteed that Mrs. Stratton's dinner should be the finest ever seen in Sutphen. And thus it came to pass that with a heart lightened of responsibility, but weighted with some apprehension as to the amount of the final bill, Mrs. Stratton had tripped away from Simonson's. Her last word, an afterthought upon the sidewalk, which she returned to the shop to deliver, was to enjoin upon the glib caterer absolute silence regarding every detail of her arrangements.

When the day arrived that was to see the triplicated entertainment of the Englishman, Sutphen was at fever-heat. So much had popular imagination expected of the object of all these

"MR. BLUDGEON HAD BETTER BE READ THAN SEEN."

cares, it was a distinct disappointment when a solemn little black-a-vised man carrying an American "dress-suit" case, stepped out of the omnibus of the Dixon House and requested of the clerk of that hostelry one of his one-dollar rooms. Barring a further demand for hot water in a jug—which the bell boy took to indicate some intention toward a private brew of punch—there was nothing to distinguish the great genius from an ordinary commercial traveler. Some enterprising spirits who had been hanging around the hotel corridor to see this arrival, went home and confided to wives and daughters their opinion that Mr. Bludgeon had better be read than seen. And these ladies who for days had been conning well-thumbed volumes of his writings sighed the sigh of discomfiture—feeling rather glad, however, that certain entertainers who were at that moment yearning for his arrival, were destined to share their disillusionment. Just before the arrival of her twelve guests for luncheon, Miss Bennett received a hasty note from Mrs. Stratton, expressing deepest regret that her fatigue resulting from necessary cares of state and home (of which naturally there was no one to relieve *her*) would prevent her from being present.

"'A positively raging headache,' she says,"

remarked Cornelia, compressing her lips. "Never mind, mother; I don't care. I'll send right over and fill up with little Miss James, the elocution teacher. She is pretty and clever, and can talk up to Annetta any day, if she only gets the chance. And if you'll believe *me*, mother, it's not so much headache the matter with Annetta as vexation because I'm to skim the cream off the milk pan first. Good gracious! I'm tired to death myself, but I'd rather die than give up now."

Curiosity among Miss Bennett's *invités* was fully sated when, upon the arrival of the guest of honor, luncheon was at once announced, and they filed into the well-remembered dining-room, where they had of old partaken of feasts of the frizzled beef and scrambled egg description. Here, *mirabile dictu!* was a board set out in modern conventional fashion—a silver wine-cooler full of roses in the center, silver dishlets holding salted almonds, bonbons and little cakes around it; at each cover a name card, napkin, glass for claret, another for sauterne, and still another for sherry, setting off a plate of blue Meissen porcelain!

So far Mr. Bludgeon had said little beside "hum!" and "ha!" He had devoured his bread and bouillon in silence, and had drank a glass of white wine; but now he bestowed upon the listening public his first connected utterance:

"Hum! ha! very fair imitation," he said to his hostess, turning his plate upside down to gaze upon the trade-mark on the bottom. "We use this kind of thing in our own house for every day. Perhaps you knew—but it may be only chance—that this is my favorite pattern in china. Looks clean and tidy somehow, so I tell my wife."

Sustained by this mark of approval, Miss Bennett inwardly blessed Simonson, who, looking unconscious in an evening dress suit, was occupied at the side table, in dispensing platters of fish croquettes to his two subordinates to serve. She only wished that Annetta Stratton might have been near enough to hear. The rest of the meal, whisked along expeditiously by the trained minions, went so fast, that Miss Bennett could hardly believe her good luck when all was over. True to the instincts of more artless days, she had some thoughts of putting on her bonnet and running out to talk it over with Annetta. But her feet ached, her dress felt too tight, her mother was fretting over the loss of both pairs of spectacles, Simonson's men were overrunning everything, Mr. Bludgeon had gone away without more than the scantest recognition of her personality—so she went up to her bedroom and had a hearty, nervous cry.

In the Lyceum Hall that afternoon, wnere the literary club met at 4 P.M. for the "lecture," everybody was buzzing over the reports of the Bennetts' swell luncheon. Mrs. Chauncey Stratton, who had insisted upon calling at the Dixon House to fetch Mr. Bludgeon to the hall in her own carriage, did not arrive till too late to hear the gossip. Just before the solemn little man stepped upon the platform, the great lady of Sutphen passed up the middle aisle, wearing a bonnet with plumes turning to all points of the compass, a trailing skirt of rich satin, a jet cuirass, and a large bouquet of violets in the bosom of her gown. Smiling, nodding on all sides with conscious pride, this patron of letters took her seat beside Mrs. Mark Grindstone.

"Seems to me you've 'picked up' since lunch time," observed that lady, in her customary muffled tones.

"I *do* feel better," said Mrs. Stratton, unable to cease bowing, although in conversation with her friend. "So you were at poor Cornelia's little affair? Do tell me how it went off."

"Six courses—three wines—the whole thing served by Simonson—couldn't have been better done," answered Mrs. Grindstone, lightly.

"Simonson?" The shot had gone home.

"Mr. Bludgeon was most agreeable. He particularly noticed the table service, and seemed so pleased," went on Mrs. Grindstone, who had a long score to settle. "But hush! Here he comes. What do you suppose he is going to read?"

"Didn't you see the program?" asked Annetta in a chilly tone. "It was settled with me, by letter. In fact I selected the extracts from his own works, and it will be sure to be satisfactory to all."

We pass over the somewhat subduing effect upon a large mixed audience, alien to him by birth and training, of the Englishman's recital of his own gems of thought. The usual frost accompanying this species of entertainment was deepened while his tragic scenes and interludes were rehearsed successively. Some members of the Club were rash enough to whisper between themselves that the entertainment wasn't worth the appropriation from their treasury required to meet its cost.

During the "tea" with introductions, that followed, Mrs. Stratton again rose to the occasion. As the fairy godmother of Genius she was immense. But Genius remained from first to last unsmiling. Life was real, life was earnest to him during that episode of American homage.

Seated at Mrs. Stratton's right hand, at dinner in her pleasant dining-room, Mr. Bludgeon, in evening dress, unfolding his napkin, looked almost amiable. When he caught sight of the soup plate succeeding the one on which his oysters had been served, his face actually expanded into a smile.

"Very nice, very nice, upon my word," he said, indicating the object before him with a condescending wave of his hand. "I had always been told you Americans do things in very lavish style, but, this, really, is more than I could have expected, don't you know?"

Annetta was radiant, although she could not exactly understand why her guest's gratitude for courtesy extended took this form. Evidently Simonson's china, silver, roses, bonbons, decorations, were on a scale surpassing anything in Bludgeon's previous experience of America. She felt she could afford then and there to forgive Cornelia Bennett for having had Simonson for lunch.

The dinner, rather a weight upon the Sutphenites, dragged heavily along, but it ended at last, and after coffee and cigars (Simonson's cigars!) the gentlemen rejoined the ladies in the drawing-room.

"I am sorry to say," explained Mrs. Stratton

to her guest-in-chief, "that as we in Sutphen keep rather early hours, the reception given for you at my friend Mrs. Grindstone's will have already begun. Mr. and Mrs. Grindstone left some time ago, with apologies to you. It is too bad that we should have to deprive ourselves of you; but I hope you will not quite forget our home and our little efforts to be agreeable."

"No, I shall not, by George," exclaimed the author, who had become a trifle more relaxed; "and when I tell them at home about it, they will hardly believe me, don't you know!"

This put the apex upon Mrs. Stratton's pyramid of joy. In her own carriage, the author seated beside her, facing her husband and Cornelia Bennett, they drove to Mrs. Grindstone's house on the outskirts of the town.

The most novel revelation of Mrs. Grindstone's party, at first sight, was that all the gas jets in the house were lighted and blazing—reckless of the monthly gas bill. This was something unprecedented, as also the cloak-room (Simonson's invention), the white-capped maids (Simonson's), and the four pieces of music hidden by Simonson in a bower of palms on the stairway. Only the familiar stooping figure of old Mr. Grindstone in his worn frock coat with a large new white silk tie, brought the public to a realizing sense of where they were. If Simonson could have tucked away the host into the hall closet, along with superfluous wraps, umbrellas, and old overshoes, that functuary would have been very much relieved.

Mrs. Grindstone, on the contrary, who might always be reckoned upon to come out strong in the matter of finery, wore a brave new gown of black silk and net, upon which had been let loose a whole collection of green beaded butterflies. The splendor of this reality at once effaced the tradition of the velvet cloak. Mrs. Grindstone's flaxen gray hair strained to the summit of her head, was there surmounted by an aigrette of green feathers, caught by a diamond brooch. Directly she saw her, Mrs. Stratton knew why her friend had hurried home at the conclusion of the dinner. Mrs. Grindstone had not been willing to expend the first blush of success of such a toilette upon another woman's entertainment.

"Isn't she splendid?" whispered Cornelia. "No such dressing has ever been seen in Sutphen, in my time."

"If I didn't feel sure Mr. Bludgeon would think it overdone," said Annetta, shrugging.

But she was herself impressed, and greatly. The revolt of Cornelia and Mrs. Grindstone from her rule; their blossoming forth with all this magnificence of a day; the fact that they would henceforth stand side by side with *her* in the reminiscences of how Sutphen welcomed Mr. Timothy Bludgeon to its Literary bosom, made Annetta smart. The one consoling thought was that Mr. Bludgeon had told her his people at home would not believe him when he described to them her dinner.

"Now for the fried oysters and ice cream," thought Mrs. Chauncey Stratton when, later on, old Mr. Grindstone offered his arm to her to follow Mrs. Grindstone and Mr. Bludgeon into supper.

Here a new surprise—one greater than all the rest—awaited her. Little tables, an innovation undreamt of in simple Sutphen, were dotting the whole room. At the chief one of these, the two leading couples, flanked by Cornelia Bennett and Major Gooch, were placed. In a trice, that indefatigable Simonson had begun the service of a supper in courses, closely resembling Miss Cornelia Bennett's lunch.

Annetta could have cried with annoyance. Not only were the dishes, the silver, the candelabra, and all the rest, just what had twice already that day appeared before the Englishman—but the china—the imitation "onion pattern"—was identically the same.

Mr. Bludgeon, when this latter fact became manifest to his observation, smiled for the second time in Sutphen. It was not, at best, a gay, hilarious, or even a complaisant smile; but a reluctant smile of flattered vanity impossible to mistake. Presently, when they called upon him for a speech, he arose holding in his hand a glass of Simonson's (American) champagne. What he said, preliminary to the gist of his remarks, Mrs. Stratton hardly understood. Her brain was tingling with vexation, she even snapped at Cornelia in an undertone, and fairly turned the cold shoulder on Mrs. Grindstone. When she could at last control herself sufficiently to be able to listen, the author had reached the climax of his sentences, and Mrs. Stratton was rewarded for all her labors in behalf of the Literary Club, by hearing this:

"Before I came to this country," said the solemn little man, "I may have had doubts about American hospitality. Since visiting Sutphen especially, I have none remaining. You are the most gracious hosts in the world. As an instance of this fact, I shall always cite my unparalleled experience to-day. At the luncheon of your Secretary, the amiable lady who sits at the table with me here, pleased me with her china service; I happened to tell her it reminded me

"NEED I SAY THAT IT GOES TO MY INMOST "

of home. What was my surprise and gratification to find that your accomplished President, at whose house I was dining a few hours later on—to whom no doubt my remark had been repeated—had at such very short notice managed to duplicate the set of china I had commended. And now, again, what can I say? Words indeed fail me, when at the hospitable board of your admirable Treasurer, I find a third set of my favorite porcelain. The resources of you Americans really do surprise me. Such a compliment, so conceived, so carried out, has never been paid to me, before. Need I say that it goes to my inmost—"

Mr. Bludgeon stopped. He had heard a giggle of hilarity that could no longer be repressed. The company, among whom Simonson and his belongings had of course been under free discussion ever since they had sat down to the tables, fairly exploded with delight.

Mr. Bludgeon hemmed, hawed, colored—finally took his seat. Mrs. Stratton hastily left the room. Mrs. Grindstone and Miss Bennett, sat on, mute, unrevealing as two Sphinxes—but evidently not offended beyond hope of recovery.

Some time after Mr. Bludgeon's visit to Sutphen had begun to pass into tradition, poor

Simonson's establishment in Main Street was shut up. He had dragged along for some time; but, lacking customers, finally decided to pack up his onion-pattern china, and the rest, and had emigrated to a more promising field for a cater-er's operations. The day of his great success had proved his Waterloo.

Mrs. Grindstone is now the President of the Sutphen Literary Club—*vice* Mrs. Chauncey Stratton resigned and gone abroad. Miss Bennett is still the Secretary. Mr. Grindstone's gas bills remain reasonably low.

LEANDER OF BETSY'S PRIDE

LEANDER OF BETSY'S PRIDE

The close of a long, bright summer's day at one of the Virginian watering-places found a little party of young people, most of them from the North, importuning jolly old Dick Ross (an off-spring of the soil, and imbued with its traditions as an orange-flower is with scent) to tell them "stories."

Ross, a tall, high-stepping, grizzled veteran, who had come out of the civil strife a Brigadier-General of Confederate Volunteers, and the hero of a hundred daring adventures about which he kept close as an oyster, was considered by the bevy who now surrounded him the best boon of their visit to the South. But for General Ross it had been passing dull at the staid old mountain spa, whither their respective families had journeyed for health and pleasure. Evening after evening, after they had danced together in the moldering old drawing-room, or played cards around a rickety table, seated in shabby chairs of defaced mahogany with ancient haircloth seats, or yawned because there was nothing else to do, the apparition of the General's lean figure strolling into their hall of pleasures had been hailed with delight. Through him the visitors had become familiar with habits, customs, and incidents of a bygone generation, in a community as foreign to their own modes of thought as if it had been geographically remote, like Russia or the golden India. And on his side Ross never realized what a tremendously old fogy he had become till he saw the impersonal nature of the approval expressed of him and his narrations in the eyes of that pretty Puritan, little Miss Eunice Hall of Boston.

She was a scion of a famous abolition tree. Her progenitors had fought to the death against Ross and his fellow-Virginians, and had triumphed loftily over the eternal downfall of the slave aristocracy in the crash of war. True, her brother Angus, named for the sturdy representative of their line who had done most mischief to the South, showed but a homeopathically diluted remnant of his ancestor's spirit in this respect. He had but a dim general idea of the part his grandsire had played in the Senate of the United States before the war, and was rather bored when accosted about it by strangers. He was more interested in his yacht, in golf, and in

University boat-races than in musty discussions and wrangles about the right of men to hold their brother men enslaved.

Eunice was different. Lately, since she had come to womanhood, it had been her "fad" to unearth every item concerning this mighty question that had rent asunder for a time the great country she revered. Since her mamma had elected to take a cure at a placid Virginian water-ing-place Eunice had found several good opportunities to prosecute her researches—but none, on the whole, as satisfactory as those afforded by General Richard Ross.

The old bachelor had been absent for a few days, having ridden away astride of a pair of venerable saddle-bags on a fiery, half-broken colt to visit some kinsfolks of whom he vaguely spoke as residing "up in the country." Now, on his return to the "Old Blue," as these springs were generically termed, General Ross consumed a hasty supper, endued himself in a suit of spotless white duck, brushed his back hair well to the front, and stepped into the parlor, where he knew the young ladies were to be found. He was received as a hero come home from the wars.

"We have stagnated since you left," said Louisa Stapleton of New York. "While Eunice

filled up her note-book with yarns of your skir-
mishing, there has been nothing for the rest of
us to do."

"I am too much honored," said the General,
bowing to Miss Hall, hand on heart. "But have
there been no new arrivals, no younger men to
push me into the background?"

"Only one newcomer," said Eunice, making
place for him on a rusty sofa.

"And he a foreigner, ailing and married,"
added Louisa, disdainfully. "Who but Eunice
would have looked twice at that old fossil with
one foot in the grave?"

"He interested me, I don't know why," confessed Miss Hall. "I met him first walking in
Chinquepin Hollow, his head sunk on his breast,
talking to himself. I thought I never saw such
a wreck of a handsome man. And his eyes,
when he fixed them on me in passing, burned
like live coals."

Old Dick started irrepressibly.

"He—you met—oh, impossible! Gad, I believe I'm possessed by one idea. A foreigner,
you say—traveling with his wife?"

"Yes; they stopped here but a day, to take
the evening train. As it happened, they had the
room next to mine, on the upper gallery; and as
our windows, opening at the floor, almost

106

touched, I heard them speaking to each other in French in a very excited, agitated way. Fearing I might overhear what was not intended for my ear, I got up and stepped out upon the gallery. Immediately there was silence, and a long, emaciated hand, like yellow wax, drew in their shutters close together."

A burst of laughter followed this narration.

"Trust Eunice for hatching mystery," said Louisa, laughing. "I saw the couple getting into the stage to go to the station: he, a prosaic invalid, his head wrapped in a silk muffler; she, a dumpy little French woman, perfectly commonplace. Come, General Ross, have you not brought back to us from your travels a new story?"

"Something that happened before the war, in a nice, gone-to-seed family," added Louisa's younger sister, Blanche. "And pray let the house have wainscoting and a secret chamber."

"No, no; something real. A war story," said young Harry Lemist, who had a thirst for active movement and little imagination.

"Upon my word," said the General, when they allowed him to reply, "I am almost afraid to tell you what occurred in the room I slept in night before last, for fear you will think I have trumped it up to answer Miss Blanche's requisition."

"How awfully jolly," exclaimed Louisa Stapleton, pulling out the fringe of curls upon her forehead.

"It was nothing of the kind, Miss Stapleton. In point of fact it was about as disagreeable an experience as I remember. But to tell the tale connectedly I shall have to go back many, many years, to the time when the old mansion that sheltered me night before last was in its prime of hospitable attraction for every one that strayed within its gates. About a day's ride from here is 'Betsey's Pride,' for by this quaint appellation is still known the house built for his young wife by a wealthy Virginian land-owner, just before this century came in."

"Not old enough by half," exclaimed Blanche, pouting.

"Truth will out, however," answered the narrator, accustomed to lawless interruptions. "It is a fine old house built like Lee's birthplace, Stratford, in the form of a letter H. The cross of the H is a large salon, now absolutely bare of furniture. At the juncture of each wing with the house arises a pile of chimneys, serving to support a pavilion on the roof, where in old days a darky band used to play for the gentry, of an evening. There was a fish-pond up there, too, in my boyhood; and there still is, at the back of the house, an old ruined garden. When a lad I loved nothing better than a visit in vacation to 'Betsey's Pride.' The oldest son of this house was my chum at the University, and also a kinsman, though remote. We will call him, for dramatic purposes, Llewellyn Chester. Chester was always a handsome, easy-going, free-handed fellow, brought up to consider himself the master of abundant means. His people gave him the best education of the times, and in due course sent him to travel abroad, attended only by the 'boy,' who in old Virginian fashion had been told off at a very tender age from among the slaves to wait on him. Leander Jameson was the 'boy's' name. Smile if you will, young ladies, but gentle and simple, white and colored, we Virginians always relish fine-sounding names. Leander was a very light mulatto, tall, erect, manly, good-looking as his master, and of astonishing versatility of talent. He could sing, whistle, impersonate any one on the plantation, was an adept in athletic exercises, and had, as we said, the manners of a prince. Chester, dependent on him for so many long years for companionship, treated him with lavish indulgence and generosity. While they were in Paris, where Leander was, of course, received as an equal by his class among the whites, Chester had him take lessons in singing, dancing, fencing, and the like; filled his pockets with money, and turned him loose upon what, as it seems, was a very wild career for both of them.

"When, a few years before the war broke out, I again visited 'Betsey's Pride,' it was to see a woeful change in the circumstances of the returned prodigal, my cousin. Chester's parents had died, his sisters had lived on there in seclusion, little knowing that his extravagance had wasted all his own and involved their substance. When he finally turned up again, like a bad penny, at their home, it was to linger a few months and die. In his last illness poor Llewellyn was nursed by Leander as no one else could have nursed him. Such fidelity, tenderness! Well, it's not of that I started out to tell. Llew Chester under the cedars of the family burying-ground, his sisters had to hear that they were ruined in fortune. But, then or since, those two women would never hear a word said against 'poor Llew.'

"Here comes in,'' went on the General, doughtily, "a chapter fortunately not common among the slave-holding families of those days. As the negroes on large plantations went on multiplying and exacting care and outlay, the revenues of their owners were naturally consumed. But it was part of our religion to hold fast to the trust committed to us by our fathers. Nothing but dire want ever made a Virginian of 'the real sort' part with a slave for money. When dire want came, so much the worse for slave and master. It was 'a degradation that bowed down the seller to the earth with shame— to have to part with these people of our black families. If anybody ever tells you to the contrary, Miss Eunice, send him to me to be convinced.''

The General, growing red in the face, winked, gulped, got up and walked up and down the room, tugged at his mustache, then sat down.

''I suppose none of you ever heard of the character as much avoided in the society of decent men with us as the headsman is in France—the negro broker and trader. But there he was, often growing fat and rich on the proceeds of his horrid business; and, like the headsman, when occasion demanded he turned up. Chester had slighted in public one of the most formidable of this fraternity, a man named Israel Johns, a sullen bully, who laid up the slight in silence and bided his time for revenge.

''As it happened, Johns's opportunity did not come till the breath had left his enemy's body. When it was known that the Misses Chester

would be forced to part with all of their 'likely'
black people, in order to pay the debts of the
estate and live, the deepest feeling was everywhere shown for the pair. My own mother went
a two days' journey on horseback to weep with
them. Remember, the oversupply of slaves in
Virginia made their buyers very particular to
select the best, and it was therefore much feared
by the friends of the family that the first man to
go off would be Leander Jameson."

"His master's friend—intimate! Oh, infa-
mous! I would have starved first!" cried out
Eunice, a red spot glowing in either cheek.

"God knows I think so, too, Miss Eunice,"
said the old soldier, bowing his head sadly.
"But that such things were was part of our burden and our curse.

"A number of us," he went on presently, "old
friends and neighbors, met together and made a
purse to buy in Leander for the estate. But
we were tricked—outbidden—overruled. The
man who got him was, as you may surmise, none
other than Israel Johns. We learned afterward
that Johns said he would own that nigger if it
took every cent he had. I can see him now, the
dirty blackguard! A middle-sized, low-browed,
swart, powerful fellow, dark as a Spaniard, with
thick lips, curly black hair, and black, shifty

eyes that couldn't look you in the face. It was at the county court-house on New Year's Day where the auction had taken place. When Leander found out who had become his owner his eyes glared like a savage animal's. I never saw a handsome young face so transformed by rage and despair. A man who stood next to me said carelessly, 'By Jove! it's he that looks like the master, and Johns like the man, I am thinking.'

"I will pass over the feelings of all concerned when, in a few days, we heard that Johns had started for New Orleans to sell his prize to the highest bidder. I for one do not enjoy analyses of human emotion under stress. When you know that Chester had promised to free Leander in order to enable the fellow to go back and marry a Creole girl from Martinique whom he had met in Paris, and had died without doing so, you see how the affair stood. What followed is well known to many persons. Johns flaunted down to New Orleans with his chattel; and on the way Leander conceived one of the most daring schemes that was ever carried out to a successful ending. He managed to get his master drunk, and on arriving at New Orleans to actually sell him for a thousand dollars to a buyer before whom Leander had posed as a Virginian

planter on his travels, encumbered with a tipsy
ruffian he was glad to dispose of cheap.

"The complexion, good manners, educated
voice, and easy diction of Leander made this
thing possible. Upon receiving, as was agreed,
the money down, he at once disappeared; and
he has never been heard of since."

"And Johns? What became of him?" asked
the hearers in concert.

"When he came to himself and found out his
condition he fought, blustered, was overcome
and held in servitude. Finally the law allowed
him to institute 'a freedom suit'; and after
many disappointments and delays he was identified as Israel Johns by persons sent from Virginia
to New Orleans for that purpose, at Johns's expense. By the time his freedom was secured and
he was restored to his privileges as a white citi-
zen, Leander Jameson was far beyond reach of
his vengeance. But Johns's spirit was broken,
and a year later he died."

"Is all that true?" asked Eunice Hall, who
had listened in breathless interest.

"To the best of my belief, yes; you may see
certainly that the tale is unvarnished by me.
But as I told you, it was only the prelude to a
personal experience of mine during the last six
and thirty hours. When, night before last, I

reached 'Betsey's Pride' after a long day in the saddle, I was kindly greeted by the two little Miss Chesters, who continue to live there in the most 'frugal way. War, that left over their heads the shell of their father's mansion, has left them but little else besides. My visit was, in rude fact, one of investigation—to see whether the two ladies were supplied with the necessaries of life, for which they are too proud to ask their friends. After a meal and a conversation that I can't think of without a feeling like a knife thrust into the heart, they showed me to my room. It was, as I at once saw, the apartment in which their brother Llewellyn had breathed his last, a cold, bare place, the arrangement of its furniture unchanged in all these weary years. Through a crack widened around the window-frame ivy had shot into the room and was curling about the inner sash. The Miss Chesters could not bear to remove this vine. 'It looked so sweet,' they said, 'growing in poor Llew's room.' An old negro woman, who brought me a jug of spring-water, hurried out as soon as she had deposited her burden. By the look in her face I knew she believed the place to contain another presence than my own.''

''Now we are coming to the real thing!'' exclaimed light-hearted Blanche, clapping her hands gleefully.

"It might be, if I knew how to dress it up in fine words at awesome intervals; but I can't. I can just tell you the simple truth—that, awakening in the middle of the night I saw, in the moonlight, as plainly as I see you now, the face and figure of Leander Jameson."

"Good gracious!" cried Eunice, sitting bolt upright, and fixing upon old Dick a fascinated gaze.

"Of course, I had been thinking of him and his master when I fell asleep. Of course, it was an optical illusion," added the old man. "I have said so to myself a dozen times since it happened."

"What did you do? What did he do?" queried the listeners in unison.

They could not decide whether or not the General was trying to take them in. But all the same, the girls clutched at each other's hands, and the young men essayed to put on an air of incredulous superiority as they waited for the climax.

"Frankly speaking," said the hero of many fights with flesh and blood, "*I* pulled the clothes over my head. *He* executed the usual 'vanishing act.' When I looked again he was gone.

The only occupant of the room beside myself was a rat that seemed to be dragging my boot across the boards of the floor."

"Was the window open?"

"Wide," said the General; "and, as it was the usual French window upon the ground floor of a bachelor's wing, nothing could have been easier for a ghost than to step in and out over the sill. Next morning I examined the premises, but on the soft old green sward of a century that came close to the window outside found no trace of footsteps. The birds were singing in the very room with me; the warm sunshine bathed its every nook and corner. A young heifer, stray-ing up, looked as if she meant to step over the threshold, but desisted. There was no trace or filament of visitation, supernatural or otherwise."

"Naturally, since you dreamed it," said Mr. Harry Lemist, convincingly.

"Naturally," said the General. "I, too, made up my mind to that view of the case. But the whole thing was a curious episode. It brought back the details of my poor friend's life and death, and of his valet's reckless and suc-cessful stroke for freedom. On my ride back here to-day I have been recalling many instances of the intercourse between Chester and Leander Jameson—things I had long forgotten. One was

that, as lads, Chester had his 'boy' learn tattoo-
ing of an old sailor in the neighborhood. The
first result of his accomplishment was the shield
of Virginia in blue on Chester's forearm—'*Sic
semper tyrannis*' and the rest of it, buried with
him, of course—while Leander carried through
life, on the outside of his right hand, the crimson image of the swan that is the Chester crest."

Eunice Hall, self-contained little being that
she was, gave at this a galvanic start.

"Why!" she exclaimed, growing pale with
excitement, "I have seen it—that hand marked
with a crimson swan—only a little while ago!
It was the one thrust out to draw in the shutters
of the Frenchman's window. I noticed it particularly."

"By George—then it *was* Leander!" cried the
General, springing to his feet.

The best efforts of General Ross to trace the
fugitive and his wife resulted only in finding that
they had boarded a train bound northward, and
were by then probably safely in New York, if
not, as seemed likely, on the ocean sailing back
to Leander Jameson's adopted home. That
the ex-slave had prospered in circumstances his
appearance and surroundings left no room to
doubt. The General's idea that, broken in

health and knowing himself to be a dying man, Leander had not been able to resist a secret visit to the scene of his birth and of his early tragedy was considered the correct one.

General Dick Ross still makes his annual visit to drink the waters of "Old Blue." The only time he has been persuaded to cross Mason and Dixon's line, to pursue his investigations of society, was for the purpose of attending the marriage of Miss Eunice Hall, when that charming enthusiast decided upon concentrating her efforts at reform of the human race upon a single undefended man.

THE THREE MISSES BENEDICT
AT YALE

THE THREE MISSES BENEDICT
AT YALE

A heavy fall of snow upon the old streets of
New Haven had not succeeded in blocking the
wheels of progress of that merriest season of the
collegiate year, known to the university world as
"Prom Week." For three days a crowd of fair
visitors and their chaperons had trod the round
of gayeties; had frequented the concerts, ger-
mans, teas, and receptions; they were now drawing breath and gathering energy for the last
crucial test of physical endurance, the ball called
the Junior Promenade.

For, to properly celebrate this time-honored
and brilliant affair, custom decrees that the list
of thirty or more dances and intermissions printed
upon the ball-card presented to each damsel
crossing the threshold of this hall of raptures
shall, long beforehand, have been filled with
names by the brother, cousin, or admirer having
the list in charge. It follows naturally that by
the time not only all these dances are accom-

plished but every "intermission" has been spent in an impromptu dance to the music of the band, alternating with the orchestra, night has brightened into dawn.

When the girls are finally induced by their exhausted matrons to withdraw from the giddy whirl, they leave behind a set of men, wild-eyed, and wilted as to shirt-fronts, cuffs, and collars, but undaunted in spirit. These men, the givers of the ball, then go away to their dormitories to snatch an hour or two of slumber before chapel, which has, not infrequently, been attended by beings in ulsters worn over evening clothes. It was to such tireless devotees rather invigorating than depressing to see snowflakes come trooping down upon the final scenes of their three-days' gayety. Toward nine o'clock P. M. the streets were encumbered by lumbering old hacks pulling up before doors to receive their loads of hooded and cloaked figures, then driving with them at a furious pace to the door of the armory where the "Prom" is given, and dashing off again to secure new fares. The drivers of these vehicles, known by name to most of the students, extend to the university and its doings an almost parental indulgence. To the guests who are aiding to make the occasion brilliant they are suave beyond imagination; solicitous of comfort,

THE THREE MISSES BENEDICT AT YALE.

descending from their perches to open the carriage doors, and assisting parlously at the elbow of the lady entering or getting out. Little of the evening's fun is to be theirs, honest fellows, but they are sustained through the chilly vigils of the night by *esprit de corps* and a brave desire to keep up the credit of their town.

Quite early in the fray one of these hacks disgorged under the armory's awning a party consisting of a mother, two daughters, and a girl cousin, all three of the young women marked with the same general characteristics of family, but differing in feature and degree of beauty. The mother, a stout, comely body, with diamond butterflies quivering about the base of a tall, black aigrette that, springing from her hair, swept the carriage top as she sat, emerged with a look denoting resolution to carry on the struggle of spirit against flesh to the bitter end. For was not her only son, her pride and joy, leader of the revels as head of the floor committee of the "Prom"? Not for worlds would she have given up the wearying privilege of sitting out the ball. Never, in her own palmiest days, had she drawn near. to a scene of gayety with a more proud sense of identification than to-night, when she shone in the reflected glory of her handsome boy!

Jack Benedict was, on his part, modest, as
becomes the truly great! An immense favorite
with his class, he had been one of those fellows
who sail serenely through college life, winning,
without apparent effort, honors toiled for by
others without success. A good scholar, an
athlete of renown, frank, cordial, sympathetic,
he was put forward by the vote of his comrades
whenever opportunity occurred to represent
them before the world; the election to his present post being upon one of these occasions.

Fresh-faced, clear-eyed, smiling, dressed in
immaculate attire, the tall young hero advanced
to meet his mother and, giving her his arm, conducted the party along the length of the large
hall to a box fitted up for the friends of the committee of management. The girls following
them were immediately surrounded by a throng
of men, consulting their dance programmes and
receiving with pride their compliments upon the
charming arrangements of the hall. It had
already been decided among the opinion-makers
that the three Misses Benedict were the stars of
the festive week, and their approbation of the
scene was generally awaited.

The vast inclosure of the armory was lined to
its arched roof with breadths of semi-transpar-
ent stuff, alternatively pale lavender and yellow

in tint, giving it a delightfully fresh and blos-somy effect. From the ceiling, lighted by veiled electric bulbs, depended a racing-shell filled with flowers and a floral football, emblems of the University's late prowess in the athletic world. From high stands on either side of the hall the band, or else the orchestra, clashed forth unceasingly enlivening strains. Beneath one or the other of these draped eyries were seen to disappear during the progress of the ball panting and perspiring men, who went away wilted after saltatory toil—but returned arrayed in the glory of fresh linen, white collars, and cuffs immaculate. Around the walls, hung with tapestry and placques of flowers, were ranged the boxes severally sold at auction to the high-est bidder among the classmen who desired thus proudly to extol the ladies of their visiting fam-ilies and parties. In these dainty nooks were assembled treasures from many a college sitting-room. Easy-chairs, rugs, lamps, draperies, tables, cushions—above all, cushions!—of every size, material, and color, were brought hither by their owners or borrowers from acquiescent friends, to make resting-places for the chaper-ons, and, when possible, the girls.

The wide, crash-covered floor, soon covered with whirling figures, became a dazzling kaleidoscope. The suggestion presented by the sight was one of extraordinary brilliancy and lightness. It was as if the Genius of American youth were abroad and at his best. No face there that did not gleam with happiness, no foot that did not spring with rapturous life. Of those encumbrances of an ordinary ball-room, the sad, the sour, the world-weary, the middle-aged, none was discernible. The young men and maidens prominent in this function, gathered from far and near in the broad Republic, were types of blended races, or pure Americans such as one may hardly see elsewhere in an Eastern festivity; and the conventional uniformity of a dance in New York, Boston, or Philadelphia was thus most agreeably varied. And through all was apparent to older eyes the joy of living and being that comes only in the first quarter of the century of life.

"Are you satisfied with it, madre?" asked Benedict, as he stopped in his evening's toil to bend affectionately over his mother, where she sat in front of the committee-box, her satin and jet rustling in the breeze created by an ostrich-feathered fan.

"Satisfied? Indeed I am! It is a perfectly enchanting scene," said the biased critic. "And your decorations are really admirable. I never

saw such a well-managed dance. But, my dearest boy, can't you sit down and take a moment's
rest? You will really wear yourself out.''

"No fear of that," quoth Jack, inflating his
broad chest. "After to-night we shall all lapse
into 'innocuous desuetude,' and there'll be full
time to repose. I hope you and the other moth-
ers can hold out. You won't see much of your
charges, I'm afraid.''

Mrs. Benedict laughed cheerily. "Dear me,
no; they only rush back to be pinned or put to
rights, and are off again. As to keeping the
faces, much less the names, of their partners in
mind, I can't pretend to do it. Agnes and Margaret, being older, take it with more composure,
but Lou flies about as if she were on wings
instead of high heels. It was a whim of Agnes
and Margaret to come dressed alike in those
blue satin gowns with the chiffon ruffles, and I
must say they are becoming. I am proud of our
dear girls' looks, aren't you?''

"I should think so," said Jack, starting with
something of a blush as she repeated this query.
He had been straining his gaze over the revolving crowd, in the effort to identify not his sisters,
Lou and Margaret—pretty blonde girls of
eighteen and twenty—but his cousin Agnes, a
tall and rather stately young woman, a year

older than Margaret, whom he had his own private reasons for not allowing to get far out of his sight or thoughts.

Agnes, the orphan daughter of a good-for-nothing cousin of Mr. Benedict's, had a year or two before, after the death of her father, been taken by these kindly people to reside under their roof in New York. When it was Jack had first owned to himself that he loved her he could not exactly say. But her clear, pale beauty, the soft luster of her hazel eyes, her somewhat foreign grace of speech and manner—born of wide wanderings in Continental cities—had begun by captivating his imagination, and ended by exciting his enthusiastic affection. Now he thought no vision of his future was complete without Agnes installed in its penetralia. And as yet she had no idea of it.

Knowing that his parents would disapprove of love-making between the cousins until Jack had at least been long enough out of college to see his way clear to an independence, he had had the rare strength of mind to keep his passion to himself. Not even his mother suspected what a cable had been thrown out to annex her bonny craft to this landing-stage for life!

One person only had shared in his secret, and he a classmate bound to Jack by the most intimate of college ties, the man of all others in the University whom Jack most admired and trusted. This was Hubert Russell, who, coming a stranger to Yale from his birthplace in a far Western town, had remained an enigma to the many, although treasured by the few who had found him out. Russell was known as a brilliant scholar, but had never been called a "grind." His isolation seemed to be a thing of preference.

To the society of women his objection was apparently insuperable. No threshold in the hospitable town had been crossed by him for social purposes. Jack Benedict, who alone seemed to exercise over him the magnetism that drew him from his shell, had often talked to Russell about his own family, and had striven without success to induce his friend to visit them in the holidays. Russell had listened with a sort of fascinated reserve to Benedict's happy boyish confidences, but had not responded to them in kind until one evening in junior year over their pipes in Jack's sitting-room. Then he had blurted out a sad tale of his father's disgrace and imprisonment and death in the penitentiary, following the embezzlement of trust-funds confided to his keeping. This awful chapter had left upon the boy's mind an indelible imprint. To remove the effect of it his mother had strained every nerve to send him to an Eastern University. At the beginning of freshman year he had lost his mother, too; and since then the spell of darkness had reassumed its sway over Hubert Russell. Benedict, a wholesome, happy fellow, born to no great inheritance of riches, and having his own way to hew in the world's wilderness, then set himself to the task of restoring Russell's tone of mind and of dissipating in him the uncertainty as to his right of place among people of unblemished honor and respectability. Little by little he had succeeded in bringing about this result. In his zeal to win Russell's full confidence he had poured out his own—had even told him of his love for the radiant cousin, Agnes Benedict, whom Jack hoped one day to win for his wife.

During the past days of gayety Russell had been more miserably shy and reserved than ever. In vain had Jack urged him to call upon or make acquaintance with his family. As a last resort he had gone to Russell's room that afternoon, and had shot into the letter-slit upon the locked door a note inclosing a ticket for the "Prom," begging Hubert to look in at the ball, if only for a glance in passing, at Jack's people in their box. While Jack now stopped to speak to his mother he saw, with curious elation and surprise, Russell standing a little distance away, talking with one of the tutors. Before he had time to beckon his friend, his sister Louisa and their cousin Agnes hurried together into the box, forsaking each the young man who had escorted her, to have some trifling repair to her toilette made by Mrs. Benedict.

"Oh, Jack!" exclaimed his madcap sister, "I am too happy for anything, and Agnes should be, if she is not, for she has evidently captivated the best-looking man in the room—next to you, of course—that tall, dark one over there. He has done nothing but gaze after her in a moony, melancholy way, while *I* am dying to know him. Do fetch him here *now*, and introduce him, there's a dear. Only give me half a chance and I can make him forget Agnes, I'll promise you."

"That?" said Jack, identifying at last the individual she was trying to point out, and watching for the effect of his revelation upon his family. "I am not surprised that you want to know him. That is my best friend, Hubert Russell."

"Is *that* Russell?" said the three women in concert. To them he had long been a household word.

"Yes, and he came here to please me, dear old chap. The trouble is, I don't know whether he'll have the courage to follow it up by being presented to you.''

"Lou does not know why he was so interested in Agnes—my Agnes," he added to himself, striving to repress the exultation of his heart as he looked upon her he loved.

II

Jack did not realize that his friend Russell could have any confusion of mind as to which of the three Misses Benedict was the cousin honored by preference undeclared. The fact was that Hubert had strayed into the whirl of the "Prom" for, indeed, nothing but to please his friend. While making up his mind to take his courage in two hands and seek for an introduction, Russell had espied, standing in a set of lancers, a girl who then and there struck him as his ideal of scarce acknowledged dreams of woman's loveliness. So swift yet strong was the impression thus received that Russell gasped and wondered what had come over him. The blood of young manhood surging into his temples showed him in a flash that he was to the full as weak as those at whom he had often jeered—Jack Benedict, for example, whose ravings over his pretty cousin had often made Russell smile with superiority and amusement. Whatever had been Russell's ambitions and hopes for the future, woman had had no part in them. And yet, here in the twinkling of an eye, the waving coils of a maiden's loosely bound hair, her airy grace, her supple, slender waist and noble shoulders had held him captive. When she turned and he saw that her face was as lovely as her form, Russell had actually started to go away. What evil spell had fallen upon him to lure his steps into this place? He resented Jack's influence, secretly objurgated Jack's tiresome lady-love and sisters, vowed he must and would return home— and lingered.

When the set was over, and the girl went off with her partner, Russell, half-ashamed, asked the college official who had accosted him if he knew who was the young lady in pale blue with a small wreath of white roses perched sidewise upon her hair.

"Let me see," said the flattered tutor, squinting his eyes to take in the receding figure. "Isn't that—yes, of course it is—a sister of Benedict's? I met them yesterday at Mrs. Clarkson's tea. But you ought to know Benedict's people better than I do, Russell."

"You know I am a recluse," said Russell, coloring.

"Then I advise you to repair neglected opportunities and make their acquaintance on the spot. There's another one—a little, jolly, laughing girl, and a cousin—not so good-looking by a long shot, but nice manners and intelligent. Decidedly, Benedict's party has lent luster to the week."

Before Mr. Grampion had finished his chuckling remarks Russell had melted away from him, and stood alone, irresolute. In this attitude he was overhauled by Benedict, who, breathless, laid a hand upon his shoulder.

"Here you are, you old fraud; come along and be presented to my mother. She is all anxiety to meet you. Expects you to have wings and a harp, from my description. And the girls are, luckily, all in the box for a minute's breathing spell. I call this kind, Russell, for you to turn up here after all, and I'll not forget it in a hurry."

Russell, having no alternative, rushed blindly upon his fate. How could he tell Benedict that he had already, without reason, without excuse, fallen in love with Jack's beautiful sister, and knew that the better part of wisdom was to retire from the fray before matters should get worse. He walked, dream-like, beside his friend, went through the ceremony of introduction to Jack's mother, received a kind hand-shake from Mrs. Benedict, and scarcely venturing to look up, heard Jack say:

"Mr. Russell, my sisters, my cousin—all Miss

Benedicts; so you will have no trouble in knowing how to address them."

Jack's voice thrilled with affection for his friend. Russell's fingers clasped in succession three gloved right hands. He knew by intuition when he touched those of the girl whose charm had enthralled him and, looking her full in the eyes, met in return a glance of gentle approbation.

"Jack has cried me in their market better than I knew," he thought, gratefully. By the immediate departure of the other two young ladies in answer to the inspiriting strains of the "Washington Post," set to a two-step, together with Jack's flight in search of his own partner, Russell found himself for a moment alone with the Miss Benedict he most admired.

"I am not detaining you?" he asked, nervously.

"Not at all. In fact, I am stranded upon your hands. My idea is that the man I promised this dance to is fainting somewhere on the outskirts of the crowd. When I saw him last he was already pumped, and supper not yet served," she answered, laughing.

"I hope they will not revive him," said Russell, yielding for once to the temptation of the hour.

Back of the committee box was a little room set apart for wraps and *tête-à-têtes*, into which he had the hardihood to invite his companion to retire, hoping thus to seclude her from the observation of her tardy dancer.

"Yes, do go; I shan't tell," said Mrs. Benedict, smiling approval. "The little rest will do you good, and I know Jack will think well of your change of comrades."

Thus everything conspired to bring closer around poor Russell the net he had not sought to weave. Sitting back among the cloaks and hats, with the music floating in to them in softened cadence, he could feast his eyes upon the beauty that had ensnared him. Her talk, bright, friendly, unaffected, girlish, was exactly calculated to win him from his habitual attitude of reserve. He found himself pouring out upon her ear the stream of strong original thought and language which had first made Jack Benedict his ardent admirer. She, in turn, felt a sense of pleasure and bedazzlement in this man's society that she had never known before. All Jack had said of Hubert Russell was more than confirmed by her talk with him; and before the brief period of their isolation was ended, something of the same everyday marvel worked upon him by her was accomplished in her gentle breast by him.

A tremor of admiration, of preference for his society, ran through her veins. She asked herself timorously what *should* she do if she never met him again; why fate had been so long in granting to her this experience of delight!

An invasion of young men (the missing partner, full of apologies for the accident of his detention, and the man to whom the next intermission was promised) broke up their *tête-à-tête*. Russell hardly believed his good fortune when she said, in a vexed aside:

"There, now, they have spoiled the best of the evening for me. I am sure we shall have no other chance to talk."

"You are going to-morrow?" he murmured, trying to seem indifferent.

"Yes, at eleven. I am so sorry," she answered in the same vein of restrained feeling.

"I *must* see you once more," he said, briefly— then drew within himself, frightened at his own audacity.

After that he watched her from afar, not being able to bring himself to join the throng of chatterers who surrounded her in the intervals of dancing or at supper time. Once only, Jack, running upon him, paused under the weight of official cares to say, brightly:

"You took to them, then? My people, I mean."

"I should say I did. They are all delightful, and your sister, Jack, is—well—"

"Which sister?" interrogated his friend, merrily.

"I actually do not know," said Russell, shamefacedly. "But she wears blue and has a wreath of white roses."

"That's my sister Margaret. Do you know I always had an idea that you would hit it off with Margaret. She doesn't let herself out to everybody by any means. But, Hubert, you might say one word for my own particular goddess— Agnes—who is the chief woman in the world for me, though I daren't tell her so till I'm farther ahead in fortune."

"Agnes? Which is she?" answered Russell, confusedly, conscious that he had given thought only to the companion of his talk in the committee-room.

"Stupid!" laughed Jack, pulled this way and that by people asking him questions. "There's but one Agnes, as I said, and she—er—she wears blue."

He was torn away by an imperative demand for the floor manager, and Russell felt relieved.

"I should not like to have confessed to him that neither of the others made the least impression upon my sensibility. I saw, of course, that there were two young females of pleasing but conventional exterior—that was all. Only the blindness of a brother could overlook the fact that Margaret is far and away the most distinguished, individual, high-bred, graceful, gracious, of the three. A man who has once spoken to Margaret would seek conversation with the other two only when he had absolutely no chance with Margaret."

Russell stayed till daylight, looking in at the armory windows, drove the last dancers to withdraw. Poor Mrs. Benedict, yawning dismally behind the ostrich-feather fan, had to confess herself beaten by sheer fatigue. Walking stiffly out upon the arm of her son, she soon fell into the corner of her carriage, thanking heaven that Jack could by no possibility be again the floor manager of a Junior "Prom." All around her limp figures were seen slinking into retreat. The most indefatigable of the dancers among the men revealed foreheads streaked with matted hair, staring eyes, shirt-fronts and collars flaccid for want of starch, buttonhole bouquets like crushed vegetables. Upon that stage of the annual festivity it were well to let fall a veil!

When Russell appeared at the carriage door to aid Jack in putting his family into their vehicle, a faint blush came into the clear pale cheeks of his companion in the talk of a few hours before.

"Might I—would you take a little stroll with me before you leave?" he ventured, with throbbing heart, to ask her.

"To-morrow? I mean, to-day?" she queried, a little confused.

"Yes; you see it is my only chance."

"I will be waiting in the little reception-room of the hotel at ten," she said, rapidly. It seemed to her that they were in a boat being borne onward by the current.

Jack and Russell walked together back to their dormitory building, where each man occupied with a room-mate a suite of two bedrooms and a sitting-room. As the gray of the sky warmed with rose color, Jack yawned mightily between two puffs at a cigar.

"I'd give a kingdom for a solid eight hours' sleep," he said, stretching his arms out. "But alas! I've got to be up betimes at the station, on duty, putting 'them' in the train, you know, or I think I'd take 'cuts' enough to tide me over a half a day in bed."

"That is one of those things I can't do for you, or I would," said Russell. "I mean putting the ladies in the train."

"Why, man, are you made of iron and whale-bone that you show not a sign of somnolence?" asked Jack.

"Not in the least. I never so heartily wished that I were constructed after that model as since this evening's experience. But remember that you have danced many miles, while I've merely hung around on the outskirts."

"You sound gay as a lark. What's come over you? I'd advise a ball a week at this rate. Perhaps you are going to come out as a 'fusser'—a regular squire of dames—in your old age."

"No such good luck. I have seen but one dame I should care to squire, and she—well—" and Russell sighed genuinely.

"A confession?" exclaimed Jack, gleefully. "But it's never too late to mend, so go ahead."

"I have no story. I am simply the victim of overwhelming circumstances. Love came un-sought, unsent, and it will probably expire when I do. So no more at present from yours idiot-ically."

"I know you too well to press queries. You will, as usual, just shut your jaw and glare in silence if you don't care to hold forth on any topic. I, too, am ready for silence, though for a grosser reason."

They kept pace together without speaking,

until they reached the landing where Jack turned in at his door, Russell ascending higher.

"Good night! Good day!" said Jack as they parted. "By the way, I forgot to mention that my mother tells me it was Agnes—my Agnes, you know—and not my sister Margaret, with whom you had that chat in the committee-room. Now, I did suppose that even a churlish old bach like you could tell the difference between those two. Margaret's a nice girl—a dear girl—but Agnes—well, you know what I think of Agnes!"

"Agnes?" repeated Russell, almost in a whisper.

"Yes, my bride-to-be, when I get money enough to claim her. My mother said she as evidently took to you as you did to her. That's as it should be, old chap. When I'm awake we'll have a jolly long talk over her perfections. Meantime, you evidently need sleep as much as I do. I never saw such a pale face as you've got on you suddenly. Brace up, and good-by till we meet again."

"Agnes," repeated Russell, mechanically, as he crept up his flight of stairs and went into his room.

Down fell his card-castle! The havoc wrought on him by that one short talk must be borne in silence and lived down. It was Jack's lady-love that he had coveted. To follow up the advantage he could not but feel that what he had gained with her would mean treachery to Jack. Rather than betray his friend he would so cancel his engagement to meet her at ten o'clock that she, considering him a boor, would not choose to hold speech with him again. He would simply fail to go to her hotel; and, cost him what it might, this course were better than undermining Jack.

III

As the hour of her appointment with Hubert Russell passed without sign or token from him, a blush of shame dyed the cheek of Agnes Benedict. She wondered at herself for making this engagement to meet Jack's friend, and for feeling ashamed to speak of it to her family. But with a sort of desperate faith in him she waited in the little reception-room at the foot of the hotel stairs where she had promised to be found. When she could wait no longer she went into her room and burst into tears. Mortified by her want of self-control, she promised herself that Russell would yet explain satisfactorily the slight to her. At the station, where Jack finally appeared—arriving at a gallop in a cab just as the train was about to start—she experienced a new pang of disappointment. Not only was Hubert Russell nowhere to be seen, but he had sent no message. Agnes came to the swift, maidenly conclusion that it was because she had cheapened herself by making an appointment to see him alone after but a half-hour's acquaint-

ance.   She would bear her punishment in silence,
and tell nobody—Jack, least of all.

As the days wore on, Agnes felt that something
had gone out of her life—something not quite
warranted by the briefness of that interlude at
the ball.   Try as she might, she could not forget
Russell and the emotion he had caused in and
had seemed to feel for her.   Jack's letters home
spoke of him as winning new honors in the college course.   When June came the family went
up again to Yale to hear the speaking for the
"De Forest" medal, for which both Jack and
Russell were to be competitors.   It was known
that popular opinion inclined to select Jack Benedict as the prize-winner, but that Russell was
considered a close second.   In their zeal for
their own hero the Benedicts were beginning to
look a little frigidly upon Jack's opponent.   And
it is safe to say that all of them, save Agnes,
hoped and prayed that Russell might not win.

Agnes, who would have given anything for an
excuse to stay away, found none.   The appointed
day saw her one of an audience assembled within
the walls of the old college chapel, whose prim
Puritan interior made even this gala occasion
seem a little less cheerful than a funeral elsewhere.   She had been standing with her cousins
in the corridor as the procession of senior class-

men in caps and gowns filed by; and, to her utter discomfiture, a momentary halt in the line had brought her face to face with Hubert Russell. In an instant the blood rushed into her cheeks. Russell, looking her full in the face, saluted her with conventional reserve. In reality he felt more of inward excitement than did she. A moment more and they had parted, she to sit gathering her faculties together in one end of the pew to which the Benedicts had been assigned, and trying to believe that she had not cared a bit.

"Did you see that Mr. Russell?" whispered Louisa in her ear. "A stiff, cross-looking fellow, spite of Jack's praises. Oh, Agnes, if he and not Jack should win the 'De Forest' I could never get over it—never. I almost hate him now, don't you?"

"No-o," whispered Agnes, blushing and hesitating.

"You are too angelic. And when any one can see Jack cares more for what you think than for all the rest of us put together! At any rate, you will own that Hubert Russell is very uncivil. He has never taken the least notice of Jack's family, and considering all Jack has been to him! A man told me it is quite well known there's a cloud over Russell's family—something really dreadful, and that Jack has simply brought everybody to forget it and to treat Russell as if it had never been.''

"What Jack has done is grand, and I honor him for it,'' said Agnes. "Who dares judge a man for the sins of his father? If ever any one showed a high and noble nature in his countenance it is Hubert Russell.''

"Don't get excited,'' said Lou, teasingly. "The object isn't worth it, in my opinion. I suppose, though, you and Jack see things with the same eyes nowadays.''

"Lou, you mustn't. Jack and I are nothing but cousins—*dear* cousins,'' said Agnes, imploringly.

Mrs. Benedict, looking across Margaret, here hushed their whispers. The exercises were already under way.

When it was Jack's turn to step upon the platform, and after a courteous bow in his student's gown to the president and judges, to begin his oration, all hearts in the audience warmed toward the manly and graceful and straight-forward young fellow. His essay, well-written, carefully polished, was delivered with excellent judgment, and when he had ended and stepped down amid tremendous applause from his friends and classmen, the general verdict was that it would win the prize. Last upon the list of speakers came Hubert Russell. The rather measured applause bestowed on him as he appeared was warmed up by the individual handclapping of his friend and predecessor, Jack. Hardly a smile lighted Russell's dark and handsome face as he began. His manner, never prepossessing, seemed now under some spell or chill of indifference.

By hazard the pew in which the Benedicts were placed was well to the front, upon the lefthand side of the speaker. As Russell finally approached his peroration, his glance chanced for a moment to rest upon the glowing, inspiring, appealing countenance of a girl who leaned forward to gaze on him with her whole soul in her eyes. The effect of this was immediate. Casting aside his embarrassment, his indifference, he burst into a fervor of natural eloquence the like of which had not been heard in that spot that day, or for many a day. To Russell was given the persuasiveness of speech, the music of the voice, the flow of language, the flexibility of countenance, that combined may give interest to material of less value than was his. When he had finished the brief essay there was no question among his hearers as to who had spoken best; they yielded him the spontaneous applause that no favor to the individual can simulate. Louder and longer than any other present applauded honest Jack Benedict, who knew himself outdone.

"Why, mother, that is not like you," said Jack that evening, when he went to take supper with his family at their hotel.

Mrs. Benedict, who had been delivering herself of a few rather bitter criticisms upon the winner of the "De Forest" (news of the award to Hubert Russell had just been communicated to them by Jack), tried to smile deprecatingly, and ended by dropping a few tears.

"I know it, Jack darling. But it's because you are so much more to us than any Mr. Russell."

"Oh, mother dear, that's the fortune of war. Russell did it a thousand times better than ever I could have done. When you think he has no one—absolutely no human being to whom to telegraph his success, and I have all of you—you will see that what I have is more than a balance for Hubert's luck to-day."

"Poor fellow! I wish he had come here with you. I wish we could say something nice to him," said the good lady, her little fit of ill-temper dissipated by native kindness of heart.

"He can't be captured, I'm afraid. He is

more queer than ever regarding women since the Prom. About that time he let me think he was or had been hopelessly in love, and was ashamed of himself for being so. Had he confided in me, I should keep my lips sealed. But no! Hubert Russell lives and must always live, I fear, severely within himself."

A secret love for some one that must govern all his life! Agnes, listening, felt her heart sink in very shame. Since she had heard Russell speak, her fancy for him, that had but lain dormant, had sprung up in full growth and vigor. And now she was told that he whom she loved in secret cared nothing at all for her. That meeting on going into chapel but confirmed her in this conviction. She little knew that a glimpse of her face it was which had inspired his brilliant effort of oratory. She little knew—

After supper, in the cool, soft evening air of June, they walked over to the town green, and while Mrs. Benedict and Margaret sat together on a bench talking, Lou strolled in one direction, accompanied by a certain young man who had of late begun to arrest her butterfly attention, while Agnes and Jack took another path.

The latter pair talked long and easily together, of the interests shared by them through relationship and intimacy of habit. It was only when Jack began insensibly to glide into the tone of tenderness she had noticed often of late with some alarm that his cousin drew back a little in her friendly attitude.

"Don't Jack; there's a dear boy," she said, coaxingly. "If you only knew how nice you can be when you are sensible."

Jack's reply was a burst of long repressed devotion, to which Agnes listened in dismay. She had no idea matters had gone so far, and was shocked at this evidence of deep feeling.

Very gently, very tenderly, she pleaded with him to give up the idea, and after a long and painful talk brought herself to the point of avowing that her love was not hers to give. Jack, who knew most of her acquaintances, could not conceive of a rival among them. But the double blow of losing in one day the cherished hopes of two such prizes was more than the poor fellow could meet with equanimity. In their absorption, as they walked to and fro, neither observed that Russell, straying out to be alone beneath the starlight with his own swelling emotions, had encountered them; had made an irrepressible movement toward Agnes, then, seeing the expression of Jack's face, had hurried on with a bitterness of jealousy in his heart that robbed success of all its charms.

"AND WITH GLOOM IN HIS HEART HE WENT BACK TO HIS
LONELY ROOM AND LIFE."

"Then you care for some one else?" Jack was saying in a fierce undertone.

"Jack—don't, please!" murmured she, tears welling into her eyes.

"But I must know," he went on, hardly aware of his own insistence.

"Yes," she said at last, never so faintly. "But he does not care for me."

All of Jack's manhood answered to this pitiful confession. He spoke to her gently, soothingly, laid her hand in his arm, and told her he would always watch over her like a brother. And Agnes, reassured, looked up in his face with loving gratitude.

At this point, Russell, on the return, again passed them. A single glance at the couple convinced him that Jack had won a prize dearer far than the one his friend had that day wrested from him.

"It was a miserable delusion of my vanity," Russell said within himself, "that made me answer to the inspiration of her gaze. It is Jack, the fortunate, the pet of Destiny, who is to claim her. Here endeth the chapter of my folly."

And with gloom in his heart he went back into his lonely room and life.

IV

Three years after the brief episode of Hubert Russell's two meetings with Agnes Benedict he found himself enjoying a hard-earned holiday in camp on an island in Georgian Bay. Since graduating, he had made a quick climb up the ladder of success. A series of fortunate circumstances had enabled him to conquer difficulties apparently insuperable. His residence in a progressive town of the Middle West, congenial occupation, and the sense of work well bestowed, had done much to restore the healthy tone of his mind, biased to melancholy through another's crime. He had corresponded intermittently with Jack Benedict, but without touching upon the subject of Jack's domestic or sentimental ties. He had read, in the "society" columns of certain New York newspapers, of various occasions upon which the three Misses Bendict had appeared before the world; of their summers abroad and at home; of the marriage of Margaret; and recently of the more than amateur achievement of Agnes as the artist of some pastels displayed at an exhibition in the spring.

What he had expected to read—the announcement of her marriage with her cousin Jack—had not yet reached Russell's eye. When that event should occur, and not till then, Russell said to himself, he would give up, once and for all, the haunting witchery of Agnes Benedict's fair face. Through the mists of three years of memory it shone upon him still!

One day in August a little pleasure-yacht of light draft and dainty build (meant to thread her way between innumerable rocky islands and dally beside tempting bits of shore, rather than to brave the rough water of the open bay) passed into an inlet where its owner had decided to throw a rope over a large rock and stop to lunch!

This primitive method of anchorage was a favorite one with the owners of the Juanita, the Cartwrights, a benevolent elderly couple from New York, who, owning a summer residence upon one of the islands lower down the bay, often took their house-parties away for days of pleasuring afloat. Mr. and Mrs. Cartwright had now as their guests several young men and maidens, among them Jack Benedict, his sister Louisa, and his Cousin Agnes. All day the Juanita had run through narrow channels of pale green water, between rocky ramparts crowned with spruce and birch, around the gray flanks of which sprang from the water forests of bulrushes, sprinkled with cardinal flowers and water-lilies. As they now steered skillfully into the channel, in which it was expected to find their usual landing-place open to approach, an expression of disappointment arose from the forward deck, where gathered a little group of voyagers in the gay attire of summer on the wave.

"A camp of men! Horrid things! Why did they choose our island!" cried Lou Benedict, pouting.

A rough house-boat anchored near the shore formed the center of supplies for the camp, often replenished by a tri-weekly steam launch from the mainland. Around a fire built upon stones a party of young men were making rather bored preparations for their mid-day meal. As the whistle of the toy yacht sounded a salute they arose to their feet and came hurrying down to the water's edge, evidently not displeased at the invasion of their privacy.

"Hubert Russell!" exclaimed Benedict, joyfully, as he identified among them his old friend. "Who would have dreamed of our meeting here?"

Greetings and introductions followed, and from this point no expression was heard from the girls of disapproval of "those horrid men."

It was in truth a stalwart and good-looking band of which Russell was the leader. Mr. and Mrs. Cartwright, nominally joining forces with them for luncheon, brought joy to the hearts of these weary cooks and bottle-washers by the unpacking of a dainty meal, well served by the yacht's cook and stewards. As the party grouped itself under the shade of glimmering birches, Russell, as if through a mockery of Fate, found himself next to the lady of his dreams. The talk, at first general, subsided into chat between persons sitting at a picnic casually side by side. Russell, almost fearing to continue where he was, looked over the circle to see Jack Benedict half reclining on the moss at the feet of an extremely pretty girl in white duck, a sailor-hat tied down with a white veil half covering her face. Seeing him thus provided for, Russell had less scruple in accepting his own half-hour of joy.

He thought Agnes sweeter, more womanly, more to his taste than ever. The rare experience was his of finding one's self confirmed in a predilection after three years of total separation from the object. They talked easily, without reference to the past, without touching upon intimate topics. He fancied, without being sure, that Agnes knew the incidents of his advance since leaving college. That she had thus kept track of him was a flattery he must accept only because he was Jack's friend. When he left her, his pulses bounding with delight of her presence, Jack Benedict took him off to the roof of the yacht's deck, where they sat by the pilot-house and smoked and chatted through a long and lazy hour. During this time the rest of the party had scattered for various enterprises—exploring the waters in canoes, fishing, reading novels under the deck-awning, or lounging beneath the trees and overhanging rocks.

And as yet no word had passed Jack's lips concerning his sentimental relations with the sex. Suddenly Mrs. Cartwright's voice called up to him:

"Mr. Benedict, won't you please take a canoe and paddle up that inlet yonder in search of your cousin and Miss Clare? We shall be starting before long, and I must begin to gather my chickens under my wings."

Jack blushed as he prepared to obey the chaperon's behest.

"You will think that for an engaged man I'm rather forgetful of my treasure," he said, smiling. "I meant to tell you, Russell, that I'm to be married in October."

Russell's heart gave a despairing leap.

"Wasn't it to be expected?" he said, smiling also.

"Well—I—there were reasons why I couldn't bring myself to write to you, old chap," rejoined Jack, as he dropped lightly into the canvas canoe a deck-hand had put into the water, Russell following. "And perhaps we need not discuss it further. But I'm happier than I deserve to be, and I have won a gem of purest ray."

As they paddled rapidly around the sharp projection of rocks that had seemed to block the way ahead of them, they saw the girls' canoe in the center of a field of lily-pads bordering another one of the rocky points here so numerous in the channel. When the lily-gatherers, who had half filled their craft with masses of gleaming flowers and long, curling stems, espied the search-party, they waved them a merry welcome.

"I knew they were not fishing; she's too tender-hearted by far," exclaimed Jack, with a lover's pride.

Simultaneously the smiles vanished from his handsome face. A naphtha launch just then passing into this inlet had left behind it a swell that made the canoe containing the two girls rock perilously from side to side. Agnes, evidently recognizing the danger, sat quite still, but Edith

Clare threw herself forward with a scream and clasped her companion in her arms. The canoe, upsetting, plunged both occupants into the broad-leafed greenery, under which they sank at once out of sight.

"Can they swim?" asked Russell, quickening his stroke.

"Yes, both of them, if they are not caught below," answered Benedict, hoarsely.

Their canoe shot madly forward. Prompt as were the people in the naphtha launch in turning back to attempt rescue, they could not vie with these men in their eager effort to reach the scene of the disaster. It was soon fatally evident that while one of the young women had arisen to the surface and was keeping herself afloat, something had happened to prevent the reappearance of the other. Jack was not so quick as Hubert Russell to see that it was Agnes who was missing. With misery clutching at his heart-strings, Russell said, entreatingly:

"Let me save her for you, Jack! It will be something to pay back all you've done for me if I can put the woman I've loved ever since I first laid eyes on her into your arms again."

He could not see that Jack was not even looking toward the place where Agnes had gone down. All his thoughts were directed to the

"RUSSELL REAPPEARED, BRINGING WITH HIM THE SODDEN FORM OF AGNES."

spot whence Edith Clare called out to him to save her. "Coming, my darling; have no fear," Jack answered her, tenderly.

Russell, without an instant's further delay, dived overboard. The canoe, violently shaken, was yet steadied by the other occupant, who succeeded in reaching Edith and extricating her in safety from her perilous surroundings.

An anxious interval, and Russell reappeared, bringing with him the sodden form of Agnes, who, snared and held under water by the green serpents of the lily-stems, was quite inanimate. They got her aboard the launch and hurried back to the yacht, where poor Mrs. Cartwright received them wringing her hands over this sad ending of her day of pleasure. During the hour while Russell waited in an agony of fear on deck, Jack Benedict, who stood beside him, became for the first time aware of his friend's long ordeal of repressed feeling for Agnes.

"And I might have spared you so much of it; it was my fault; I only was to blame," Jack said, sorrowfully. "Ages ago, had I known this, I might have told you how she gently and tenderly—poor soul—but with finality, put a stop to my boy's dream of winning her. Now, when God only knows whether she will be with us in the future, I can say no more. I think, Hubert—

mind, I can't say I am sure, but I think—she must have loved you from the first."

Russell could not speak. He wrung Benedict's hand, looking at him with hollow, haggard eyes.

"So many people have known for the last two years of my attentions to Edith Clare, we have been so frequently announced by our friends to be engaged, that, even before the engagement was a fact, it did not occur to me that you, though living so far from us, were in total ignorance of our relations. You can see, Hubert, that Edith is my other self. My fancy for Agnes grew up with me, but the love for Edith came with my maturer manhood. Our engagement was announced only just before we all came off here to visit Mrs. Cartwright, or I should have written to inform you of it officially and of my approaching marriage."

"There!" exclaimed Russell, who was straining his ears to hear sounds from the little inner cabin, where Agnes lay under the care of Mrs. Cartwright and a doctor—found, fortunately, among the campers on the island. "I am sure I heard her voice."

Jack's sister Lou came out to them, her face beaming with delight. "She has stirred—has spoken; she breathes easily now," was what they heard. "In a little while, the doctor says, she will be herself again," Lou tried to add, but was choked by her excitement.

An hour or two later Russell, who had been invited by their hostess to go back with them for a little visit to her island villa, sat beside the lounging-chair of Indian bamboo heaped with rugs and cushions, in which they had placed Agnes upon deck—clad for the occasion in things they always carried aboard in a wardrobe assembled for such emergencies. The yacht was speeding merrily homeward over a track of westering sunshine. Forest fires upon the small islands along their route glowed like jewels under canopies of dense, pearly smoke. In the wake of the boat violet shadows appeared and vanished into the water. All ahead of the two was bright as the Promised Land.

What had so long seemed impossible to these lovers had come about in the simplest fashion. Their hands meeting had conveyed the joy of each at reunion with the other. A few broken words from Russell told Agnes that he had no dearer wish than to win her love. And Agnes— Now she was pouring out to him the confidences of three years past; was claiming his in return; was hanging upon his words, her face so full of happiness as to tell its own story.

"We are all avoiding that part of the deck as if it were a region of pestilence," said Lou to her future sister-in-law. "I don't think I ever saw such bare-faced love-making in public. I have had to put up a parasol so as not to see them. As for you and Jack, Edith, you may step down from your pedestal as fiancés. Although mamma will be very much taken by surprise to hear that Agnes has come up into these remote waters to annex a young man from off an island, I think Jack will induce her to feel resigned. Certainly, Russell is a fine, manly fellow. From all I can see, I fancy there will soon be only one Miss Benedict."

"And for how long will there be even one?" asked Edith, teasingly.

Lou blushed, and would not answer.

A GIRL OF THE PERIOD

167

A GIRL OF THE PERIOD

A great deal of feeble sympathy was expressed for the Foljambes when it became known they had lost their money. But regret for that sort of misfortune to one's neighbors is always tempered when they have previously shone before the world as the dispensers of extravagant hospitality. Thrifty, self-centered people who have been inconspicuous because of their objection to amusing society at the expense of their own purses, are apt, under similar circumstances, to receive much more hearty condolence. The Foljambes, father, mother, sons, and daughters, invitations to whose parties had been scrambled for in New York and Newport, during several seasons past, were now reaping the harvest of over-abundant giving.

It was generally agreed that Mrs. Foljambe, a weak, silly woman with a bee in her bonnet for fashionable life, had quite long enough enjoyed her place in the fierce light that beats upon the throne of American plutocracy. The

father, a clever financier, with the one social
accomplishment of effacing himself when the
strain of recognizing his individuality became
too great upon the frequenters of his house, was
dismissed with even scanter consideration. The
sons—one recently started in business, the other
but just out of college—were very little known
except to their cronies. The real stars of the
Foljambe family, those whose effulgence or
eclipse was likely to be of consequence in the
social firmament, were the daughters, Lilian
and Olive.

Of Lilian, the elder, it had been customary to
say that in a matrimonial point of view she
might be expected to do "anything." Beautiful,
accomplished, fine of grain, cradled and bred in
polished luxury, she was the traditional princess
who could not sleep for the crumpled roseleaf
in her couch of down. Since she had made her
appearance before the world her friends had
watched, open-mouthed, to see who would
carry off the prize. Of the half a dozen men
prominently in her train, none could be adjudged
exactly fit for her. "Dancing men and dips"—
meaning diplomats—was the way they were
summed up. Of course it was not to be expected that a mere diner-out and frequenter of
cotillons—a man whose boast it was not to have

missed a ball or banquet during the season—
could presume to mate with this very choice
specimen of the leading set in Manhattan's
aristocracy. Lilian Foljambe was destined to
high place, name, fame, and representative position. She was of the stuff—declared some
enthusiasts—of which the wives of our ambassa-
dors to foreign courts should be made. Though
if ever there was a head for which nature
intended a tiara—inherited, not bought—it was
Lilian Foljambe's.

But Lilian had come to be four-and-twenty—
an age in woman when the insolence of youth
must needs begin to curb itself and look about
to reckon the comparative values of its chances
for actual establishment in life, without realizing
any of the hopes fixed upon her. She had,
needless to say, her full complement of unemotional offers from the kind of young men whom
she met nightly wearing evening dress with white
waistcoats, who talked afterward at the club
together concerning their ill-luck with her, and
wondered "what the deuce the girl was waitin'
for." She went abroad year after year with
her family, was presented at various courts,
made many titled acquaintances, was extolled
for her good looks, and reputed to have twice
her actual fortune. And still there was no hint

of the "great match,". or of any kind of a match, for the fair Miss Foljambe.

Olive, on the contrary, with not half Lilian's beauty or style or grand air, had at twenty-one her quiver full of admirers who would have liked to be something more. Olive's chief possessions were a brown skin, a pair of laughing hazel eyes, a bewitching mouth and teeth, plenty of common sense, a merry nature, and a nimble wit. During her first winter "out" she had announced to her family her intention to marry Stephen Luttridge, a clever young architect, who had nothing in particular a year. Mrs. Foljambe—ranking the outcome of Luttridge's profession, together with those of art and literature, as in some way connected with food cooked in chafing-dishes and a maid-servant receiving cards between thumb and finger—looked honestly alarmed. She induced her husband to declare that he would give nothing "down" with either daughter unless she should marry to please her parents.

Olive smilingly declared that she could very well afford to wait until Luttridge should have three thousand a year, at which time she meant to take the matter into her own hands. Mr. Foljambe, egged on by his wife, had stipulated that the affair should not be called an engagement.   And Olive had answered, laughing, that she did not care what they called it, provided no other girl got Stephen Luttridge.

Now a crash had come.   Foljambe's name, hitherto most familiar to a set of men who had confidence in his probity and were dazzled by his schemes, had been seen of late in every newspaper in connection with the story of his stupendous, over-confident, and rash speculations.   And such a tremendous failure had not been chronicled in years!   It was a curious fact that the men who commented on it said generally, in conclusion, "If he could only have gone on for one week longer, by George, he'd have been safe!"

Foljambe was not afraid to meet his creditors. He had chosen a trusty and capable friend to be his assignee for their benefit, and was sure he could more than pay his debts—though his remaining assets were not all of a kind to be immediately turned into cash, and he could hardly expect much of a surplus for himself. Indeed, nobody else expected his assignee to be even able to satisfy the creditors; and so his credit, even with his friends, was entirely gone. He had given to his sons good educations with which to fight the world on their own account— for most young Americans a more fatherly benefaction than a balance at a bank and leisure to haunt clubs. And they were manly young fellows. It was, in plain words, his womenkind of whom Martin Foljambe was afraid.

His wife, with whom he had begun life in the narrowest fashion—who had helped herself with both hands to the accretions of his successful business career—would never, he knew, be able to forgive the folly of his downfall. With women of her type, to have is to forget all previous deficiencies, to claim prosperity as a right, to resent reverses as a personal wrong. Sweet, beautiful Lilian, who was the poetry of his prosy existence, she would be gentle and forbearing with him. But Lilian, deprived of her luxuries, was an image he could not bear to contemplate. He knew her to be so utterly unfitted for the world of work-a-day. Olive, now, was in some way different. She, like her sister, had been an extravagant little puss. But Olive had a way of pulling herself together and facing contingencies that gave him more hope for her endurance of the change.

Those were sad days in the great stately house off the Park, and so well known to the world of fashion, following the Foljambe failure. The large staff of servants was prompt to desert the sinking ship. A buxom kitchen-maid officiated over the copper stew-pans of the departed chef. Mrs. Foljambe, in her bed with nervous prostration, in charge of a trained nurse, complained that she could not get a cup of bouillon fit to eat since Lenormand had left. Next the stables were depopulated. Then the pictures and curios and ceramics were sold at auction, and the house was offered for sale by the assignee, to whom everything had been surrendered. As there is always in the great metropolis some family stepping up to replace one that chances to step down, the agents effected a prompt "arrangement" by which the Foljambe mansion, furniture and all, passed into other ownership.

In less than two months after his misfortune Mr. Foljambe stepped out alone into the street, and looked back upon a dwelling in which he had no belongings save a couple of modest trunks and several portmanteaux to be called for by an expressman later on.

Who shall say that Martin Foljambe did not feel a lump of bitterness in his throat as he gave his final instructions to a care-taker and walked hurriedly away into the avenue whence he could no longer see his home? It had been at his wife's instigation that he had built it; she had devised, superintended, ordered everything, on a scale that outshone most of his predeces-

sors in such constructions in their neighborhood.
The only things she had not concerned herself
about were the bills. Enormous as they were,
he had paid them without a hint to her that she
must have been cheated in various quarters.
But it had been many a long year since Mrs.
Foljambe had concerned herself about the sum
total of a bill!

All—all—the fruits of his manhood's work had
been lavished at her feet, and here, when he was
wounded to the quick by the jilt Fortune, his
wife, where was she? Sailing eastward in the
best rooms of a crack ocean liner, in company
with her lovely Lilian, without whose society she
had declared it would be impossible to recover
the tone of her shattered nerves!

It was really the only thing for her to do, so
had said Mrs. Foljambe to her doctor, reminding
him of the tremendous help she had previously
derived from certain baths in Germany. The
doctor, wise in his generation and well aware of
what was expected of him, had suavely acquiesced. Mr. Foljambe was informed by his wife
that her sole chance of recovery lay in the jaunt
in question—and as to expense, it was a real
economy, he knew. The money she was to have
at her disposal was a sum of a few thousand dollars which had been given to her years before by

her husband—which he had invested for her in her own name—and which had chanced to have been never as yet spent by her. So the state-room on the ship had been taken within a day or two after she had announced to him her intention of going abroad.

Lilian, clinging to her father's neck with tears and caresses, assured him that she did not want to go; that it would be dull as ditchwater for her, and that she should always be thinking of him left behind. But Lilian was overpowered, and in due time yielded to her mother's decree that her first duty was to her.

Not so Olive. Without protestation, without gush over her father, she had calmly said she had no idea of going abroad that summer. With the help of her friend Luttridge she had picked out a little flat on the west side of the Park, where there were tree-tops for the trouble of going to the window and a delightful sense of being out-of-doors. The sale of her pearl neck-lace had paid for the furniture. She retained as cook the kitchen-maid who had been trained under M. Lenormand, and then, when all was done, announced to her father that they —he, she, and the brother recently come home from college—were going there to live, the other brother having resigned his place in New

York and gone to the West to grow up with the country.

The evening of the day that found Martin Foljambe creeping dejectedly out of his former mansion, with a heart in his bosom heavy as the iron that had seared it, brought him up-town to see for the first time Miss Olive's new arrangements for his comfort.

To Martin, past the age for picnics, the whole thing appeared but a mournful makeshift. But Olive and Luttridge, who came in to dine upon a grilled fowl and a can of mock-turtle soup, and Tom, the recent graduate, who was charged by Olive "to help to cheer papa," laughed and chaffed and made merry with the glorious unconcern of youth. After dinner, when the two young men went out into the Park to smoke their pipes, Olive sat with her father upon a sofa pinched between two doorways of their narrow sitting-room.

"And now tell me, papa," she said with alarming briskness, "just what I may expect as an allowance to keep house upon."

He explained that for the present he would have nothing he could call his own except the sum the assignee was paying him weekly for his services in assisting to wind up the assigned estate to the best possible advantage, and that, even from that, certain amounts would have to be deducted for use for things other than mere housekeeping.

"Oh, well," said she, "we shall be able to live. And do you know, I already love this. It is like a honeymoon without the bother of a husband. You will have an excellent draught of air through your bedroom. I forgot to tell you that I got a note to-day from Mrs. Louis Rushmore offering me the work on her husband's notes of that expedition they made last year to Mexico. Mrs. Rushmore started in herself to put them in shape for publication, but seems to have got into a hole. You know, it is to be a sort of 'In Memoriam' for Mr. Rushmore, published on the most lavish scale, with illustrations and all that. She recalled that when we all met in Mexico Mr. Rushmore took rather a fancy to me principally because I was the only person of the party who could read his handwriting. You remember, he got me to copy out in his note-book certain of his own memoranda that he couldn't decipher to save himself?"

"And how, pray," said Mr. Foljambe, writhing upon the hard little sofa Olive and Luttridge had thought so artistic in design, "did Mrs. Rushmore come to suppose you were in need of employment?"

"Because, daddy dear, I've been foraging around for something to do, for a month past," said the girl, frankly. "You know I am nothing if not up to date. I expected to be somebody's secretary, thanks to my good, clear handwriting. But the blessing of Mrs. Rushmore's work is that I can do most of it just here, and at the same time 'boss' the maid, who might get tired and bolt if she were left too much to herself."

"Poor Rushmore died just while he was deciding to go into San Miguel with me," remarked Mr. Foljambe. "He was one of the careful, conservative kind—while I—"

"Don't be ashamed of your spirit of daring—don't, papa; you share it liberally with me!" said Olive, gayly. "I haven't the vaguest idea of what San Miguel was or is, but I'm perfectly sure I'd have gone into it and left Mr. Rushmore trembling on the brink."

"It was one of my failures, dear—a mining speculation that promised everything, and flattened out in a year or two. If I had the money now that my holdings in that stock represent to me, it wouldn't be long before I should be out of this pit, I tell you. Until I was failing, I hardly counted the cost of it. What it has cost me amounted to a fortune in itself; and I hold—or rather my assignee for the benefit of my creditors now holds—a strong majority of the whole capital stock. But within the last few years there has been no work done in the mine except what the sale of ore extracted would pay for—which has not been much—and the stock cannot now be sold for even a penny a share. Indeed I advised the assignee to-day to sell the shares to anybody who will offer anything whatever for them, and to do it quickly, before the chap can change his mind. Olive, my child, whether you succeed or not in your Rushmore business, I'm proud of you for taking up the first work that comes to hand. But there's one thing I ought to ask—how long is Luttridge going to be satisfied to do without you?"

"Of course, papa, he was deadly foolish," said Olive, crimsoning. "He wanted to be married right away, and come in here, the saucy fellow. But I've stuck to my ultimatum of last autumn. When he gets enough to keep us without my being a drag on him, I'll say 'yes.' Just now I wouldn't leave you for all the world. Every minute of this day I've been thinking of your getting home and finding everything so nice."

Foljambe's heart reproached him for his contempt of her poor devisings. He caught his brave little woman in his arms and kissed her as he had not done in years.

Olive's interest in deciphering the Rushmore hieroglyphics grew with the continuance of her work, which daily opened out into new channels of discovery and information. Mrs. Rushmore, rejoiced to find she had not misplaced her confidence in the girl's ability, went off to Europe, leaving the whole charge of the book in Miss Olive's hands, together with a very liberal sum to be paid her in weekly installments in remuneration, and the promise of more to follow when the work should be finished. Foljambe himself, in better health and spirits for his daughter's guardian care, found that, on the whole, his enjoyment of life was rather increased than diminished. His younger son rejoiced his family by finding employment as secretary to one of his father's old friends, who was primarily to take him off for a summer of travel through the wonders of the far West. Letters from Mrs. Foljambe, while giving gratifying assurance of her physical improvement and of the usual impression made by Lilian's beauty upon casual grandees, did not now touch a sore spot in Martin's heart, for the simple reason that the wound was healing under Olive's influence.

Summer came, and Olive, at her desk heaped with dictionaries, encyclopedias, and works of reference, transferred from Mrs. Rushmore's library, had hardly time to wonder if she were herself. While all the other young women of her acquaintance were preparing gowns for their holiday campaign, going off to lovely country homes with keen zest for the outdoor life that had previously been her greatest joy, or taking wing for Europe, she in her trim cotton gown sat down by nine o'clock to spend all the morning hours in close devotion to her task in hand.

With her mental energies thus healthily astir, her faculties bent upon elucidating and compiling interesting facts, she was really happy and at her best. She could truly say that she envied no one in the world.

"After all, it's no more than you, and Stephen Luttridge, and lots of nice, clever men who deserve just as much of the pleasure of life as I do, are doing every day," she said one evening, when her father told her she was a chip of the old block as far as working was concerned. "And while you are endowing me with your attributes, daddy, give me your pluck and — something higher, please. Even if I weren't getting paid for it at the best market rates, I'd never begrudge this summer, that's brought me to know my own dear father as he is. Thank goodness, there comes Stephen to take me for a walk. All this bottled-up energy of mine is fearful if I get no physical outlet in the day. Daddy, I forgot to tell you, I've been brushing up my Spanish latterly. I've had two lessons a week from a cheap and solemn little don Stephen found for me. So many of my Mexican letters are in Spanish I found it almost necessary to know their language better. To-day my little professor made me his farewell, and we had a conversation in his own tongue that would have startled you—I really think I talked faster than he did—if not so grammatically.''

''I don't doubt it,'' replied her father, looking at her admiringly. If Olive had told him she had taken a prize for an essay in any branch of science after two months of study he would hardly have doubted her.

It was harder work when the heat of July struck the city. Olive, yielding to her father's solicitation, went off then for a week to a friend in the country, but came back determined not to try the experiment again. She was out of all touch with the people she met at the Claverings' house party. Kind as they meant to be to her, she had lost the shibboleth, the habit of thought and speech, that could make her one of their circle. And if, on her return to town, thoughts would intrude of wide, smooth-shaven emerald lawns, great forest trees parting to reveal vistas of hill

and lake, flower-beds blazoning the turf, rides
on horseback, days on the golf links, and long,
delightful country walks, she had courage to put
them aside. But all this happened to be at the
time of Luttridge's holiday; when, seeing how
much he needed change from office work, Olive
had, in her own bright, imperious way, insisted
that her lover should go off to the Maine woods
for a fortnight's fishing, without regard to her.
And Stephen, albeit reluctantly, had acquiesced.
One morning, as she sat down to her desk, the
ancient Aztecs seemed for a while to be more
than ever distressingly remote and uninteresting;
then the maid came in with a long chapter of
complaints about the iniquities of the janitor and
butcher boy. When that was over, Olive's eye
fell upon her calendar. It was the day when,
the year before, the Foljambes had been giving
their great ball at Newport, accounts of which
were cabled over sea, and had filled the atmos-
phere of the Western Hemisphere. Of what
consequence were the Foljambes now to the
world that had courted them?

"Evidently," thought Olive, dashing into her
papers, with an heroic attempt to fix her mind
upon them, "it does me no good to go a-junket-
ing. Between me and my other life a gulf is fixed
that I should be wiser not to attempt to bridge."

A ring at the gong-bell of the flat! So sharp a ring as to make her start like a guilty creature. This interruption brought her to the discovery that, for the first time since her change of abode and habit, she had been crying over "things." Katrina's arrival with a dingy card revealed the name of a Mexican, an ex-journalist, employed by Mrs. Rushmore to make certain researches of which the result was to be reported to Olive herself. In her capacity of editor, the latter had already received several communications from this Mr. Ramirez.

"But there are two," whispered Olive, who, from her little study divided by curtains from their only reception-room, could distinctly hear voices and footsteps.

"Yes, m'm; but one of the gentlemen didn't give a card. He's a—a person, m'm—not a caller, and he's jabbering away for dear life in French or Eyetalian or Rooshan, or some o' them desperate tongues, to the other one, m'm. Shall I say you'll be out directly, Miss Foljambe?"

"Yes, Katrina, and bring me a glass of water," said Olive, meekly. She was glad to remain alone for a little while, subduing her nervous fit, and swabbing the marks of tears around her eyes. In her present unwonted resentment against existing circumstances she was even inclined to eschew the ancient Aztecs and the whole splendid inheritance they have left to posterity in the New World.

"It is really the heat that has got the better of me," she thought. "But how much worse for poor Katrina in that little burning-glass of a kitchen! I am ashamed of myself. I will, positively, never do so any more."

The voices of her waiting visitors, at first subdued to the ordinary pitch of a stranger's tones upon entering an unfamiliar place, here forced themselves upon her aural consciousness. The men were speaking in Spanish, and certainly not of the matters Olive was expected to hold in common interest with Ramirez.

"It is not the first time, Juan, that you have tempted me with ventures; and they have always come to nothing. I haven't the money to spare, I tell you; and that's flat."

"There is no mistake this time, Ramirez. If I could only make you believe me! If you do not accept, I go to Señor Mores, who, when he knows the facts, will take me up quickly. Think of it! A beggarly sum in hand, we buy out the San Miguel stock from a man who does not know its value, and our fortunes are made forever."

San Miguel stock! In a flash it came to Olive that her father was the chief owner of San Miguel stock.

"Why do you think I came to New York?" went on the eager speaker. "For the pleasure of that long, bone-breaking journey across the continent, eh? Or to pass a month in this city, where a poor man is ruined by charges if he demands to eat or drink? Why did I fasten myself to you to-day, and follow you here, when you showed no desire for my company? Because I wanted to get ahead of another man who will arrive to-morrow morning. Am I to fail because you, my oldest friend, will not help me to raise the money? It is not a 'fake,' as you call it in English. I swear to you that I speak the truth. San Miguel is up, up—on the top of the wave. In two days the newspapers will have the news of their rich find. Here is a telegram I received on arrival at my hotel, a few hours since. The secret was to be kept only till Latimer, the clever man of their syndicate, should have had time to reach New York and visit Mr. Foljambe."

"Foljambe! Caramba! Hold your tongue!" hissed Ramirez.

There was a sudden hush. The conversation passed into whispers. Olive, trembling with excitement, slipped back into her bedroom, put on her hat, seized gloves and parasol, and darted out to the rear of the flat to interview Katrina.

"I cannot receive those men now, Katrina," said the young lady, breathlessly. "Give me full time to get out of their way, and then—but not until they call you—tell them I am not at home."

"It's not sneak-thieves they'd be, Miss Foljambe, and you goin' to call up the police?" the maid asked with natural emotion.

"No, no, Katrina. They will do no harm. But I cannot stop to see them. It is a matter of important business for me to attend to. Something I have found out that I must see my father about, without delay. Mind, you are on no account to give these men, if they ask for it, Mr. Foljambe's address downtown."

"Trust me, miss," said the woman, importantly. "They'd never be gettin' me to let on where they'd find the master, poor gentleman, after all the troubles he's had already."

Olive, considering every moment's delay of the men a clear gain, and reckless of the evident belief of her honest handmaiden that she was going to warn her father to flee from the myrmidons of justice, hurried out of the front door.

Katrina, anxious to fulfill the trust imposed in her, tarried inconceivably long; when Ramirez,

his patience exhausted, rang her up for the
fourth or fifth time, the woman sauntered into
the room wearing an air of defiance blended with
cunning. Between Ramirez's scant supply of
colloquial English and Katrina's voluble mysti-
fications the two men were fairly routed. The
Mexican, putting his papers upon the table,
finally beat a retreat.

But he reckoned without his enemy.

"Maybe it's me you think would be serving
yer dirty summonses upon the master!" cried
she, as, exploding with wrath, she picked up the
envelope and thrust it back on him.

"Come away, Ramirez; the creature is certainly mad," said the other, nervously. To his
mind this delay about trivialities, when he had a
fortune in his grasp, was insanity on Ramirez's
part as well.

* * * * *

Fleet of foot and full of courage, Olive sped
upon her way. Reaching the nearest station of
the elevated railway she boarded a car and fell
into a seat, looking back in actual fear of finding
herself overtaken by the two Mexicans whom
she had eluded. After all, was it not a will-o'-
the-wisp she was pursuing? As it often happened to her in acting upon impulse, the first
cool moment—though that did not come until

the train was well on the way downtown—
brought its pangs of self-distrust.

But nothing could go wrong about visiting
her own dear father and confiding in him her—
A sudden jarring of the wheels upon the rails,
a shock—what was it? Olive, together with the
other passengers in her end of the car, was shot
forward violently, all falling in a heap. Then
came a crash, a sound of shivered glass, some
screams from frightened women, and at last a
full stop—after which people picked themselves
up and wondered whether or not they were badly
hurt.

Coming around a curve they had run into the
rear end of a train stopped unexpectedly ahead
of them because of a breakdown of its engine.
There were no serious bodily injuries, but there
was much agitation and every prospect of a long
delay before the track could be cleared and the
train could proceed. Olive, the worse only for
a badly battered hat, a broken sunshade, some
damage to her clothes, and a scratch across her
brow, had her hands full for a time with pacify-
ing other more nervous women and crying children, who could not be persuaded they were not
doomed to fall into the street below.

When at last she had succeeded in getting to
the plank-walk along the side of the railway

track, and had thus, with the assistance of a train hand, reached the next station, she descended to the level of Mother Earth with her feelings somewhat dashed. In her forlorn plight she was not fit to be seen on the streets, and indeed the condition of her hat was so shocking as to make her hesitate to enter a public vehicle. There was not a cab in sight, but after a rapid walk to Broadway she discovered a great wholesale warehouse where, when she had explained that she had just been in a collision on the railway, they allowed her to purchase a cheap straw hat that was at least better than the one she discarded.

More delays! The cable-car, into which she finally got, ran along peacefully enough to just below Canal Street, where a block occurred, necessitating an attempt at possession of her soul in patience until the moments grew to feel like hours.

Unable to endure it longer, she sprang to the ground, crossing through a jam of vehicles to the sidewalk, then stood looking up and down for a cab. Everybody stared at her, until she was afraid she might be arrested upon a charge of drunkenness, because of her excitement and of her battered appearance.

Her face flamed with heat and exertion. The

wound in her forehead streaked her handkerchief
with blood. It was very near mid-day. Lacking
a parasol, the sun's ardor seemed to her more
oppressive than it had ever been before. And,
as ill-luck would have it, the passing cabs at
that hour, in midsummer, and in that portion of
the town, were so few and far between, that not
one, not already occupied, came along until she
was ready to cry with anxiety. It was the first
time she had ever been there alone.

Poor Olive felt her courage oozing out at her
finger tips. After all, would not she be laughed
at by her father as a mistaken busybody, concerning herself with affairs of which she had
no knowledge? And as the sun beat upon a
pavement swarming with alien folk who jostled
and stared at her, she almost gave up in
despair.

"You make some mistakes, my impetuous little Olive," had Stephen Luttridge said to her a
few days before they parted, "and—perhaps—
commit some follies. But your intuitions are
the keenest, your pluck the best, I have ever
seen in a woman. And I promise you now, I
am going to stand by them both, so long as we
both shall live."

How Olive had glowed with pride at her lover's
eulogy! As it here came to her memory, she

turned bravely around facing the Battery, and started to walk.

The pain in her head was growing; she felt a sensation of dizziness. In all that crowd, pressing her onward or coming to meet her, there was not a familiar face, or one to whom she could appeal.

At this moment, a blue-coated officer crossed the line of her uncertain vision. Olive ran forward, laying her hand upon his arm, and besought him to get a carriage for her. The man, scrutinizing her closely, ended—to his eternal credit, be it said—by speaking civilly.

"There's one coming now, Miss, if you think you'd be fit to drive alone. Perhaps you'd better step into a drug store till your head cools down a bit."

"Oh! no, no. I am all right, officer; I only want to get to my father's office, No. — Wall Street, please. Tell the driver to take me quickly, and I'll thank you very, very much."

Once inside the friendly hansom, Olive's courage flowed back in a full stream. For half a mile or more she lay at ease upon the cushions, fanned herself, arranged her hat and veil anew, thought of her father's kind pity for her mischances, and rejoiced in finding him—when, presto! the horse was down upon his knees and badly damaged, the passenger shooting forward, her wrist twisted in the attempt to prevent herself from falling further.

A crowd gathered about them. Olive, assisted to alight, protested that she was not hurt; and a good Samaritan, who saw the girl's pallid cheeks, led her into a neighboring doorway, summoning another cab.

"You must let me take you to your destination, though," said the gentleman who had aided her. "I happen to have daughters of my own about your age, and should be very sorry to have one of them left to shift for herself under these circumstances."

"It can't be so very far now to my father's office in Wall Street," replied Olive, suppressing the pain of her injured wrist. "I am dreadfully anxious to get to my father's place of business."

She mentioned his name, and the gentleman took off his hat—but was evidently puzzled by her forlorn appearance.

"I have good reason to know Martin Foljambe," he said, courteously. "But for his generous action a few months ago—something he need not have done, but chose to do—I should have been hard hit. My name is Whitwell, and I beg you to give yourself no further concern, Miss Foljambe. I shall surrender you safely to your father's keeping in a very little while.''

"Oh, if it is not too late!" exclaimed she, for the first time losing her self-control.

"You are late for luncheon, if that's what you mean; but I dare say Mr. Foljambe will look out for you. It is always a treat to my young women to descend upon me for their mid-day meal, and I am well broken in to supplying them.''

When they stopped before the desired building and Olive offered him her purse to pay the cab, her kind friend declined, of course, to receive it, but observed that her cheeks had again grown very white. In crossing the hall to the elevator he made her lean upon his arm, and as they shot up to the floor upon which Martin Foljambe now transacted his affairs, in the office of his assignee, her escort felt that she was trembling painfully.

"I am growing weaker," thought poor Olive to herself. "How wretched to frighten papa like this. Oh, I must not, I will not faint! I will hold out till I tell him about San Miguel.''

"Courage, my child," said Mr. Whitwell. "In one moment you'll be there.''

At the end of a long corridor they saw the names they had come in search of.

"He is in, Miss Foljambe," said the young man to whom she had put the query, "but I am sorry to say our orders are that Mr. Foljambe is not to be interrupted. He is receiving some gentlemen on important business."

"Two foreigners?" asked the girl, forcing herself to speak calmly.

"I think so, Miss Foljambe. I was out at lunch when they called, but I understood they are Spanish gentlemen, and Mr. Foljambe's orders were most explicit that he is not to be disturbed."

Olive never knew how her strength held out to march past the astonished clerk, tap at the door of her father's room, and follow this up by entering the forbidden portal. Quite two hours had passed since she had quitted her home upon her mission of warning. There had been full time for "Juan" to induce Ramirez to decide upon their plan of action, find out Mr. Foljambe's habitat downtown, and proceed without interruption to the spot.

As already stated, Foljambe had decided that the mine was worthless, and had advised his assignee to sell the San Miguel stock at whatever price it would fetch. When, therefore, the two Mexicans had appeared—offering for it a merely nominal sum, to be sure, but accompanying their proposition with the guileless explanation that, as Juan lived near the mine and had a little money, he was willing to risk something on the venture of becoming part owner of the property, though it seemed to be of no real value —Martin considered himself in luck. He thought that here was a windfall, though certainly not a large one.

While Ramirez, interpreting for his friend Juan, was in the very act of urging an immediate acceptance, so that a matter of so little importance might be closed without further bother, and while Foljambe was holding back with an attempt to prove his indifference, making excuse that the assignee would arrive presently and they could then decide the matter, Olive had burst into the room.

"I beg your pardon, papa," she said, frightened and faltering; "there has been a little accident, and I must speak to you alone."

Foljambe, much startled, put his arm around his daughter's shoulders, placed her in a chair, and requested his visitors to wait in another room until the return of the gentleman through whose hands the matter must pass. As they went out Ramirez darted upon the almost fainting girl a look of suspicion and resentment.

"What is it, my dear?" asked the father, anxiously. "What in the world has brought you down here alone, and in this condition?"

"Your friend, Mr. Whitwell, papa. He is waiting outside, I think; but never mind him or my appearance or anything, till I ask you if you have sold your San Miguel stock."

"Good heavens!" cried Martin; "and what do you know, you kitten, about San Miguel stock?"

"Only that it's up—up—on the top of the wave," she cried, breathlessly, repeating what Juan had told in her hearing to Ramirez. "That they have made a rich strike of ore. This man I saw here just now has crossed the continent at top speed to buy you out; and another person—somebody called Latimer, who, he says, is the clever man of the syndicate—will be in New York to-morrow morning for the same purpose. Oh, papa, if you have sold San Miguel it will break my heart!"

"By George, I haven't; but you were just in time!" cried Foljambe, greatly excited. "It's the closest call I ever had in all my business life. How on earth you found out, Olive, beats me. But if it's true—good heavens, child, how did you find it out?"

"They were at our house this morning—talking together in Spanish," she said, her voice beginning to sound to her further and further away—"and I remembered what you had told me about San Miguel. I started without waiting a minute to find you, but the elevated train broke down, and there was a block on the cable cars—it was very hot—then my hansom horse fell down, and I hurt my wrist—I'm afraid, papa, it's beginning to make me feel—a little weak.''

She could articulate no longer. Her words trailed off into incoherency. The long strain had been too much for her. For the first time in her life, Olive fainted dead away.

Juan and Ramirez knew their game was up—knew it before a message came to them from the room where Mr. Foljambe was occupied in restoring his daughter to consciousness, where Mr. Whitwell, summoned to come in, was explaining the circumstances of his encounter with the little heroine.

For the visit and proposition of Mr. Latimer, which occurred the morning following that of Ramirez and his friend, Mr. Foljambe was sufficiently prepared. Latimer's surprise when his offer to buy was declined outright, as was also his rapid increase of the amount first suggested as a fair equivalent for worthless stock, all this is written on the tablets of Martin Foljambe's memory. He will probably never cease chuckling over it as a pendant to his daughter's clever interference.

Olive went on with the Rushmore memorial

(which in due time appeared in print, with great credit to the editor) until her father, coming in one unbearably hot evening, gave her the welcome tidings that San Miguel had set him on his feet again.

"We shall be rich again, my girl, thanks to your grit and common-sense," he added, bending over the sofa, where she reclined, rather languid and overdone and trembling with excitement. "And about the first use I shall make of spare funds will be to set up you and Stephen. I take it, from what your mother writes, Lillian will marry that Captain Ramsdell. I don't care a hang about his being next in succession to a baronet, but I do like his asking her when he thought she had lost her money."

"The bell!" cried Olive, springing to her feet as the welcome annunciator sounded. "Glad as I am of your splendid news, papa, I am gladder still that to-night has brought Stephen back."

"I had quite forgotten that little circumstance," remarked Martin, as she flew by him like a whirlwind to meet her lover in the hall.

THE STOLEN STRADIVARIUS

THE STOLEN STRADIVARIUS

In a low chair, drawn up to secure the full light of a Welsbach burner, a little woman sat darning stockings. Although full forty years of age, she was astonishingly young and fresh. Her dark hair, twisted in a shining coil at the back of a small, well-shaped head, her rosy lips and white teeth, the look of alert interest in her hazel eyes, the plain but becomingly arranged dress, all suggested that her present condition of solitude was incidental rather than habitual.

The room in which Mrs. Blair's deft needle repaired the havoc of stalwart feet in their daily walks to and from the money-getting haunts of men, was clearly the resort of culture untainted by vulgarity. On the second floor of a small three-story dwelling in a street unknown to modern fashion, years of use as a family gathering place had toned its modest belongings into harmonious attractiveness. If the furniture was worn, it better accorded with the russet and dun hues of the old books covering half the walls; and the drawn curtains of faded crimson stuff did not rebuke the faint odor of tobacco that lingered in their folds. Above the books hung numerous good engravings, photographs, and etchings that lifted thought and piqued imagination with suggestions of the wide world's beauty and romantic history. In the most isolated corner a substantial table, littered with papers, a letter-press, a stray pipe or two, a big common-sense inkstand and writing pad, with a rack of books of reference, betrayed the snug harbor of a male brain-worker; while a stand of blossoming plants in a south window, a tea-table set with bits of quaint silver, and a couple of becushioned wicker chairs indicated a woman's idea of *dulce domum*.

This room was, in fact, the common property of a busy married pair and their busy children, who rightly considered their reunions in its pleasant precincts to be a fair equivalent for other things denied them by Dame Fortune.

The house and its furniture, with a small sum of ready money, had been the portion given to Molly Christian on her marriage, two-and-twenty years before, with Terence Blair. He was a good-looking, well-bred, clever Irishman, who, coming over to the New World to make a living out of journalism, had at once anchored himself happily by falling in love with and winning the prettiest and best-balanced girl of his acquaintance in New York.

Mr. Christian, Molly's father, after so contributing to his daughter's needs, had wisely put what remained of his fortune into an annuity that supported the amiable but unpractical gentleman until his death two years before our story opens. This disposition of his funds had been indorsed by Mr. Christian's family and friends with more satisfaction because of his previous persistency of faith in certain silver and copper mines that had given him every facility for cultivating the process known as throwing good money after bad.

Although Molly's handsome Terence had not, according to her expectation of him, quite set the world of his craft on fire, he had made a respectable livelihood; and she and their children adored him for his sweet, cheery temper and easy-going ways. Late in her life he had imported to live with them a lively little old Irish mother—styled by the juniors "Granny"—who proved to be just the dash of flavor needful to complete their family salad. Petulant, affectionate, witty, and light-hearted, Granny had bravely helped her daughter-in-law to bear the increasing burden of domestic life on a limited

income in a community where upon working people there is a call for every dollar before it is
well in hand.

As the children had grown up, and their varied
mental gifts cried aloud for the best education of
the times, Molly had, indeed, had much ado to
make both ends meet. Luckily for her, the
strain of keeping up appearances was not among
her trials.

When the Blairs had married, possessing between them means enough to give and take the
hospitality of that 'simpler period, they were a
part of the circle that in those days codified the
social laws of the metropolis. Mistress Molly,
a whilom belle of her set, did not lack for attentions, and Terence was popular. But very soon,
it became apparent to the young couple that they
were straining overmuch to keep abreast with
people who affected to put aside the hum-drum
ways of their Revolutionary, or Dutch, or Puritan ancestors; that the growing elaboration of
life among their kind must drive the Blairs either
to accept without returning, or not to accept at
all. So Molly let go the threads of gossamer
that bound her to her world, and little by little
the Blairs had drifted into insignificance. To
Terence, with his insular density as to the shades
of difference in American society, it had not

seemed a mighty matter to give up Molly's friends; but she was a woman, and at first it had cost her a few natural pangs. Now for nearly twenty years she and Terence had lived their own life, and on the whole had done very well without the things forsaken.

How was it, then, that to-night, as the little house-mother sat at her homely task, her thoughts, roving over the field of her interests, general and special, had settled with a tinge of wistfulness upon a very trivial matter? In an evening newspaper she had chanced to read the account of a ball, given the night before for the young daughter of one of her friends of early years, when the *débutante* had literally walked upon flowers.

"Lilies of the valley strewing the floor of the alcove where Tilly Beaumoris stood beside her mother to receive! And for my girl, to-night of all nights, when she plays her violin before Levitsky, not so much as a posy to wear in her best frock!" This was the arrow that pierced Mrs. Molly's armor!

Yes, it was Kathleen, bright, radiant Kathleen—her nineteen-year-old daughter, the sunshine and perfume of their home—who had begun to disturb the long-standing family peace.

What Molly had cheerfully accepted for herself, she now, like a true American parent, began to think might be bettered for Kathleen.

An hour before, she had seen the chiid—heaven in her face—set forth with her father for a musicale in the studio of an artist, who had promised to fetch there to hear her play the great Herr Levitsky himself, whose verdict made or marred an aspirant in her field. And Molly had no sort of doubt as to Kathleen's rare talent for the violin.

The only cloud upon Kathleen's horizon had been that mamma must stop behind.

Molly had pleaded—though Kathleen quite understood it to be a pious fiction—that she really could not make the effort to go to Crichton's musicale; that she was better off at home; that she would certainly be nervous, and that Kathleen would see it, and fail to play as well. Kathleen knew—and Molly knew she knew—that the frugal little lady's only remaining evening gown was too hopelessly decrepit to make another appearance in public without the renovation requiring time and outlay just then impossible to bestow on it. As for its alternate—the old black satin surviving the days of a fuller purse—that had "suffered a sea change" into modern conformity with gores, and gathers, and what not, and was at the moment rippling sheenfully

from Kathleen's own slender waist, the bodice
veiled in transparent gauze of the same somber
hue, through which the girl's white throat and
splendid shoulders gleamed with a pearly luster.

What Kathleen had done to bridge over the
insincerity of her mother's excuses, was to put
her strong, round arms about Molly's neck and
half blind her with enthusiastic kisses.

Maurice, coming a moment later into the
room—Molly's oldest son, Maurice, with his
six foot one of young manhood set off by cheap
broadcloth, speckless linen, and the ruddy hues
of health and modesty—had repeated Kathleen's
onslaught; and lastly Terence, always laggard,
wearing his high hat of ceremony, and struggling into his overcoat as he hurried in, had
kissed her good-by, and bade her be of good
cheer, since their girl was sure to do them credit.

Ah, well! What did anything matter so long
as she had these?

No, no, she did not envy her old friend, Lottie
Earl, now the important Mrs. Beaumoris of the
society newspapers, or covet ever so little that
lady's grand establishments in town and country, her yacht, her travels, and her vogue. It
had been only a silly passing fancy of Molly's
about the waste of all those lilies, because Kathleen had asked for a few to brighten her gala

toilet, and could not be gratified in view of the winter woolens needed for poor, dear Jock—who was serenely wearing his last year's rags in a snow-drift up at college!

Then merry Jock passed in review in his mother's anxious thoughts—Jock, whom the family were putting through the university by dint of constant self-denial and petty economy. And then, Maurice, whose clever drawings were beginning to be sought for by the editors; his hopes and ambitions, his loving confidence in her, flooded her heart with tender meditation. Next, Terence had his turn, and there was a space for Granny. And before all of these images of her worship, Molly poured a libation of love that made her as happy as a queen. Gone now were the barbed thoughts of a little while before. How "they" would laugh at her next day, when she confessed her feelings as to Mrs. Beaumoris, for to the Blairs most sentiments were common property. Terence, his eyes full of quizzical enjoyment, would call her a little socialist. Maurice, throwing back his head in a jolly laugh, would declare, provided the Blanks gave him Horner's new novel to illustrate, Mrs. Beaumoris was welcome to strew forty thousand lilies upon her daughter's pathway. Granny would let fly some cheerful satire, and Kathleen—well, if to-night Levitsky approved of Kathleen's playing, after this the girl would be too well satisfied with her lot in life to bestow even a transient sigh upon anything lacking!

As the clock on the mantelshelf chimed eleven Mrs. Blair started in surprise. Her stockings were all done, and piled beside her in neat rolls; and still there was time to run over those last proofs of Terence's, so that he, poor dear, might get to bed for once in decent time.

It was not for the intellectual treat that Molly Blair, her rather overtasked hazel eyes radiating contentment, next set herself, with the careful facility of one trained to the work, to read over the pile of galley slips representing part of her husband's new book on the Romance Languages, then running through the press. Truth to tell, in her zeal of sympathy she almost knew the paragraphs by heart.

So deeply immersed in her occupation was Mr. Blair's proofreader, however, that by and by, although Molly had meant to listen for the welcome sound, a latch-key was turned in the hall lock below, and she did not hear it. A moment later, a whirlwind, apparently, bore into her presence a young creature with the brightest eyes and ripest lips in the world.

"Oh! little mother, darling!" cried Kathleen,

breathlessly, "how shall I tell you my good news?
It was like a fairy tale; and Maurice thinks so,
too. He's just as glad as I am, I can see; only
we've not had time to talk it over. Well—to
begin with—*he* was there—"

"Who, Maurice?" asked Molly, happily.

"No, you teasing mother—Levitsky—and
when Mr. Crichton took me up to introduce me,
the hero just glanced me over with his cold blue
eyes, and looked about as much pleased with new
company as the real lion does at the menagerie.
Then, I began to play. And what followed I
don't know—except that the people were as still
as mice, and that I forgot even Levitsky standing there, so tall and weary, between the fold-
ing doors. And then—and then—everybody
clapped, and I played again; and, when I had
finished, papa, who was close behind me, took
my violin away. Next Levitsky came straight
through the crowd, and took me by the hand,
and said—oh! what *do* you suppose he said to
your good-for-nothing child? 'Mademoiselle,
you have all the rest, if only you persevere till
you master the technique.' His eyes were no
longer like steel; they shone on me with the
softest, friendliest gleam. That terrible golden
mane of his could never frighten me again, I
think. He was as gentle as you are, mother dear;

and there we stood talking till he left, and papa said I must come away, too."

"You will say I was, for once, fit to take care of your treasure, won't you, Molly?" supplemented Terence, who had followed the family swan upstairs. "When you see the state of excitement she is in, you will agree that if that little head isn't turned to-night she'll indeed be a lucky girl. Levitsky showed pretty plainly that it wasn't by any means a thing of every day for him to meet with the likes of her; and when *he* roared, of course all the little animals chimed in. I suppose, there'll be no living in the house with Kathleen after this."

"Oh, yes! I shall be so good, so amiable, everybody can live at peace with me," cried Kathleen, throwing off her fur-trimmed wrap and revealing her beauty to the eyes that never tired of it. "But here we are, mother, neglecting a most important duty. In the fullness of his pride, this heedless daddy of mine has gone and invited two or three men to come in here presently for supper."

"Terence!" said Mrs. Blair, reproachfully.

"It's only Malvolio, Molly dear, and little Catullus Clarke—"

"Such a beautiful new poet, Mr. Clarke is, mother, with night-black, silky hair and chiseled features—don't you remember papa's review of his book Sunday before last—here it is, this dark-green duck of a booklet, with every modern idea in the make-up—"

"But my dears, however will Mr. Catullus Clarke bring himself to consort with a Welsh rarebit?" interrupted the housekeeper, with some severity. "And to save my life, that is all I can think of to offer him."

"He'll tackle it fast enough," said Terence, comfortably. "But don't fash yourself, Molly; there'll be oysters to stew in the big chafing-dish. Maurice stopped behind us to fetch them from our old friend Felsenberg's, whose place was open and in full blast as we passed. Come downstairs now, and get things ready in the dining-room, for it isn't every day we celebrate our daughter's first step in the temple of Fame, I'd have you remember, ma'am."

"And, mother," put in Kathleen, as they adjourned below for action, "you will never guess whom I met at Crichton's! Mrs. Beaumoris and her older daughter, who is a fanatic for music."

"Lottie Beaumoris?" said Molly, remembering with a blush her envious soliloquy of a little while ago.

"Yes, you know she is by way of being a patroness of talent, and the daughter is one of the little fishes that swim after Levitsky. They were amazingly condescending to me, not in the least identifying your child. Here comes the wonderful part, mother. Mrs. Beaumoris has engaged me to play at an afternoon party on the 25th, when Levitsky's to be the star! I saw in a minute that the master had suggested me, and felt perfectly overwhelmed with thankfulness. And the price, mamma—the price I am to be paid is stunning. Perhaps Mrs. Beaumoris may not think so, for I noticed she hesitated when she offered it—but she little knew how my spirit bounded at the offer. Let me whisper, dear; I don't mean that any one else shall hear."

And bending her stately head to the level of Molly's little pink ear, she breathed into it a sum which, to the simple notions of the mother, seemed more than generous, although, as Mrs. Beaumoris afterward boasted, she was "getting this new girl for half price."

"Is Kathleen telling of her latest captive?" said Maurice, arriving with his can of oysters, to find their little dining-room aglow with warmth and comfort.

"Nonsense, Morry," said his sister.

"Yes, but it's true, she has got her net over not only the great Levitsky, but a man who can

help her on tremendously, if he chooses to.
And he does choose apparently, since he asked
me when he might call here—and by the same
token, I told him we'd be having a bit of supper
later on, and would be glad to have him drop in."

"Morry!" said both women, in a breath.

"Well, now, mother, isn't it my business to
look after Kathleen's musical interests? And
didn't Crichton tell me this fellow was no end of
a swell in musical high society? The first time
I noticed him was in the train of those Beaumoris females, who appealed to him for everything. But he couldn't take his eyes off my little
sister after she began to play."

"I never even saw him," exclaimed Kathleen.
"Or, stop! could that have been the beautiful
Raphael-faced creature who was standing be-
tween the doors during my first piece?"

"I suppose *you* might call him Raphael-faced,"
said Maurice, with a brother's fine scorn of his
sister's ʻenthusiasm for any man. "But *I*
looked at him purely in a business light, as an
impresario of young genius. He talked to me
some time, and accepted my invitation to drop
in. I don't know, now that I come to think of
it, what there is about Thorndyke, but it's something not quite—well, I give it up. Judge for
yourselves when he arrives."

And now, all was in readiness for the impromptu feast. On the hob of the grate fire, a kettle, indispensable to the impending brew of Terence's famous punch, simmered assurance of speedy boiling. Terence—trusting to no one the concoction of a Welsh rarebit, for which he had won renown at Trinity College, Dublin, now years too many ago to be mentioned — was already at work over a chafing-dish. Kathleen, her cheeks crimson, her lips of the true pomegranate tint parted with delight—a large damask napkin pinned over the front of her made-over black satin—was peeling a lemon for the punch. In this branch of culinary service she was admitted to be an adept—so thin, so even, so unbroken the golden spirals she produced!

Maurice, perched on the arm of his sister's chair, fell into lively whispering—for, to Kathleen, almost before his mother, the boy was accustomed to carry his hopes and fears. To him also that evening had fallen a stroke of good fortune. Had not he heard from Mr. Malvolio, the art-critic of the *Regulator*, that —— had spoken to him of putting the illustrations of Horner's book into the hands of "that young Blair?" And was not —— the member of the great publishing firm most to be relied upon for the distribution of covetable plums?

Mrs. Blair, glancing back as she went into the pantry to prepare for her oyster stew, thought the old clock under which her children sat—whose broad face had looked down for so many years on the councils of her family—had never seen a fresher, a more winsome pair, eager to confront the great world on their own account.

The father, affecting not to be conscious of Morry's confidence to Kathleen, recalled the days when he had peeped in on them at early morning in their nursery, to find both youngsters sitting in the same crib, with heads together and tongues wagging industriously over their forecasts for a day, then as wide and broad to them as was the future now. Neither of his children, Terence decided with satisfaction, had parted with the simple straightforwardness of that primal period.

Mr. Malvolio, whose ring startled Maurice from his perch, and sent him to open the front door, considered himself well favored in being admitted to one of Blair's little off-hand suppers. As the famous critic and dictator upon matters of pictorial art came into the room, his pallid, mask-like face, and snaky, black locks disheveled over a high forehead, suggested rather a ghost at the feast than a would-be reveler.

After him presently arrived Mr. Catullus

Clarke, whose overcoat and galoches had but just been deposited in the little hall, when a third ring made itself audible.

"That's Thorndyke, probably," said Maurice, hastening away—the maid servants of the Blair household having been long abed and slumbering.

"Maurice has asked an important stranger to join us," said Mrs. Blair, with a little air of apology to Malvolio.

"Thorndyke—I should think so," said Malvolio, but interrupted himself upon the entrance of Kathleen's "Raphael-faced" young man.

He had been going to say that Thorndyke was much oftener visible in houses of the Beaumoris variety than in the haunts of upper Bohemia, but this struck him as hardly a gracious observation, even among the easy-going Blairs.

The first appearance of the musical virtuoso confirmed, in her mother's eyes, Kathleen's description of him. There was an expression singularly unworldly and winning about his fair, handsome face. In his hand he bore a cluster of rare white orchids, fringed with maiden hair fern—"a real Beaumoris bouquet," said proud Molly to herself—which, with an almost reverential air, upon being presented to that young lady by her brother, he offered to Kathleen.

This act of public tribute from an oracle of such repute in the world where she aspired to shine filled the girl with tremulous delight. It also disposed her to think more than kindly of the giver. But Thorndyke did not follow up his advantage by pressing himself upon her further notice. He talked in turn with Terence Blair, Mrs. Blair, and Malvolio; tasted and praised Molly's oysters, declined Terence's punch, and settled down in a corner to await further developments.

At this point of the proceedings still another ring was heard—brisk, fearless, insistent, the sort of ring Jack might have caused to resound through the Giant's castle.

"Who can that be?" asked Mrs. Blair. Terence, to whom she addressed herself, did not reply in words, but, with a sly smile twinkling about his eyes and lips, referred her to Kathleen.

Kathleen, engaged in conversation with Mr. Malvolio, whose quaint drolleries of speech gave her continual pleasure, turned around with a movement half impatient, half resigned.

"Ask Morry," she said. But Maurice, quite under the spell of Mr. Thorndyke, was listening with delight to that gentleman's discourse upon some theme evidently kindling to the imagination.

"Morry *would* invite him, mother," the girl went on, with a trifle of petulance in her voice. "It is only just Colin."

"Only just Colin!" Behold a youth, tall, heavily built, powerful, his head leaning a little forward from the shoulders, his brown, healthy face adorned with the expression of good will toward mankind that, after all, is the one unfading charm of the human countenance. It was because of his trust in things that Colin never felt abashed, greeting the great and the lowly alike with honest good-fellowship. Although in the eyes of a critical woman of the world his person might have been found lacking in certain exterior signs deemed by her class indispensable, his looks and manner when he came into a room carried with them irresistible attraction. An ex-hero of the university, where Maurice had been his devoted chum and follower, the echo of Colin's achievements in athletics had not yet died out in the two years since he had graduated. Take Jock Blair, for example, at present a junior under the wing of the same alma mater, and seat him at table in Colin's company; a babbling and confident young fellow enough in ordinary society, Jock would be stricken dumb and reverent in the presence of this composite Napoleon and Wellington.

Now a hard worker in his first year at the law, not even those outsiders, chill of blood, who affect to contemn the practice of manly sports among healthy young collegians, could have found ground for a charge against Colin that he was subordinating brain to muscle. Under his new teaching, he had done more than well. To the physical animation acquired in college he had many times given thanks for helping him to endure this later life, in which a walk uptown after working hours was the chief outlet for his tremendous energy of body.

When we have said additionally that Colin was of a very short purse, and had no backing of family in New York—seeing that his relatives were unimportant residents of a small Western town—that he was hopelessly in love with Kathleen Blair, and that at college he had been dubbed Colin chiefly because his real name was John Walter Mackintosh, the tale is told.

Knowing that his charmer was that night to undergo the ordeal of proving her quality as a violinist before the supreme Herr Levitsky, our young man had moved heaven and earth to get an invitation to Crichton's musicale; having succeeded in which, he had passed through a tumult of emotions regarding a proper appearance for the occasion.

Maurice, sharing his confidence, had lent sage advice. Colin, who perhaps for no other reason would have taken on himself a debt, had secured upon the installment plan of payment a new suit of evening clothes, the genial sartor who provided them supplying, out of the fullness of his sympathy, facings for the coat of a better quality of silk than was nominated in the bond. At the instigation also of the more knowing Maurice, the aspirant had next repaired to a much advertised "Fire Sale" of "Gents' Furnishings," where he had laid in a dozen white linen ties, "imperceptibly damaged," and six hemstitched pocket handkerchiefs. This done, there was yet a mighty obstacle to overcome. For two interminable days Colin had not seen his way clear to the possession of a pair of patent leather shoes. Over and again he had surveyed wistfully his rough ordinary footwear, and reluctantly decided that it would not do. The jest of the bootmaker to whom he had ventured a remonstrance as to the high price of his wares, that it "took extra leather to cover some men's feet," was iron entering Colin's soul.

At this critical juncture, somebody had been called in haste from the law office claiming the services of Mr. Mackintosh, to draw up an old woman's death-bed will. To Colin had been assigned the task, and also, to his eternal gratitude, the small fee resulting. The speed made by him uptown that day after office hours, to reach the bootmaker before his shop should be closed, recalled to our hero some of his efforts at sprinting between hoarsely cheering crowds of college sympathizers.

Two minutes after he was invested in all his hardly-won integuments, Colin had forgotten them. He had long been planning how to present Kathleen with some flowers to wear at the musicale. Knowing her favorites, he had purchased a sheaf of those "naiad-like lilies of the vale, whom youth makes so fair, and passion so pale," at a cost that would deprive him of luncheon money for some days; then, with a strong desire to see her pleasure in them, had walked around to the Blair's house carrying the gift in person.

On the doorstep his courage had failed. Kathleen, sternly intent on checking his too rapid advance, might, and no doubt would, decline his offering. So rather miserably, the big young man had turned around again and marched away with his pasteboard box. At the corner, he bethought him of a recent speech of hers—that "better than anything but music," she loved flowers. This renewed his prowess. Again he stormed the lady's portal, and again fell away, discouraged, in apprehension of her frown. The scrutiny of a passing policeman served to weaken his last remnant of resolution.

The lilies, returning with him to his lodging, were, with continuing uncertainty, carried on to Crichton's studio. There Mr. Mackintosh, proving to be the first arrival, had judged it best to remain secluded in the cloak-room, until a number of men, passing in, gave him countenance to enter the scene of entertainment. His vague plan of contriving to intercept Kathleen on her arrival, and putting the flowers in Morry's hands, with the request that she should wear them, had now vanished into thin air. He wished at last he had never burdened himself with the confounded things.

What Colin felt while Kathleen had witched her audience with youth and loveliness and talent may be divined by the reader. Perhaps by ruffling the leaves of the book of Memory, some chronicle may still be found there, uneffaced, to suggest the proud tingling in the young man's veins! The little lock of darkest hair, that while she wielded the bow had the habit of breaking cover and falling down upon a fine jetty eyebrow, the rich flush in her cheek swept by the lashes of down-dropping eyes, the noble unconsciousness of her face and figure, thrilled him with a more passionate resolve than ever to win her for his own.

When she had finished playing, and the crowd thronged about her to indorse the master's verdict, Colin had kept aloof. He did not want to spoil the hour by commonplace; and indeed his heart was too full for utterance. Maurice, just then running upon him in the throng, had bidden his friend to supper. Colin, fed with new hope, had returned again to the dressing-room, intending to take a walk until it should be time to present himself at the Blairs'. Between two men talking over the performance of the evening as they lighted their cigars, he heard Kathleen discussed in terms that he considered daringly impertinent. Although the phrases used were chiefly those of custom upon the appearance of a new performer in her field, one of the men lent to them an emphasis so offensive that Colin had much ado to restrain himself from flying at the offender and choking him backward into a pile of hats.

Tempted to leave his now oppressive offering for beauty's shrine in Crichton's fireplace, he took up again his box of flowers and went out into the night. How far he wandered through the chill, deserted streets in the effort to make time pass ere he thought it proper to appear before his goddess, Colin did not realize. When he could bear no longer not seeing her, he had rung Mr. Blair's door-bell; but when he was asked into the supper room, where they were all assembled, the spurned and imprisoned lilies were tucked away on the lower shelf of the hat-rack, behind the galoches of Mr. Catullus Clarke.

"And where will you sit, Mr. Mackintosh?" asked Mrs. Blair, holding out a kind hand of welcome to her new guest, who accordingly dropped into the chair nearest her own.

Colin could hardly speak. In the stranger guest, ensconced in intimate conversation with Maurice, he recognized one of the men he had desired to knock down in the dressing-room at Crichton's!

"Now, we may notice in Clarke's poems," Mr. Malvolio was saying with wicked relish, "what Emerson once remarked about Oxford. 'Nothing new or true, and no matter.'"

"I do not pretend to solve my own problems, my dear fellow," returned the poet, languidly, as he lay back at ease in a large arm-chair, surveying his patent-leather toes; "I only state them to average intelligence, and then pray for the interposition of the Power that brought speech out of Balaam's ass to give understanding to some of my readers."

"Indeed, yours is the dearest little book we have had this month, Mr. Clarke," exclaimed Kathleen; "and your poster is the wildest and weirdest in my collection."

"Then I have not printed in vain, Miss Blair," answered the bardling, looking at her with admiring eyes. In reality he was entirely happy.

It was only being overlooked that ever caused Catullus pain.

"Gather your roses, while you may, Clarke," resumed Malvolio, cheerfully. "Presently the twentieth century will throw upon you mysterious folk a searchlight in which even you will stand revealed, and then your occupation will be gone. You owe Blair a debt of gratitude, by the way, for slating you so discreetly a couple of weeks ago. It's immensely clever how he manages to let his authors think the failure to appreciate lies in him only, and that the world at large is ablaze over their productions. Now, in that thing about you, for instance, the readers of book reviews—I wonder who they are?—must have thought Blair a schoolboy who had accidentally tangled an Olympic deity in the tail of his kite.

It was only after they had paid one fifty for the volume, I dare say, that they found out the truth."

"Don't spoil my wife's supper by talking shop over it," said Terence reprovingly. "To come here for the purpose of discussing modern literature—"

"You flatter Clarke," interrupted Malvolio.

"Is hardly my idea of entertainment. You might as well invite a letter-carrier to take a walk for pleasure."

"Or ask Malvolio to talk about Monet—" said Clarke.

"Who has seen 'Heart of Topaz'?" asked Terence of his guests.

"I, says the fly, with my little eye," answered Malvolio. "It is a pretty peep-show; but she is only Mrs. Tanqueray done into Japanese. If we are to have that lady at all on our stage, let her come in the strong, original guise of Pinero's heroine. Although you, my dear Miss Blair, must stay away when she appears—"

"Now *I* protest," said Mrs. Blair. "But at this rate, we shall never find a subject of conversation upon which we agree."

"I beg your pardon," exclaimed Malvolio, whose glass Terence had just filled with a steaming golden mixture of innocent appearance.

"There is one, and that one uppermost in all our minds, yet deepest in our hearts—"

"Hear, hear!" murmured Mr. Clarke.

"I need not," went on the speaker, arising and holding his glass in his right hand, while upon his saturnine countenance gleamed an attempt at angelic amiability, "say many words to emphasize the pleasure Miss Blair's triumph has given to-night to her hearers. Up to the present time, I must confess, I have known the young lady chiefly in her capacity of sub-critic to her father. On various occasions like the present, I have profited by her opinions upon the topics of the hour; and I can truly say: 'Now, by the salt wave of the Mediterranean, a sweet touch, a quick venue of wit; snip, snap, quick, and home; it rejoiceth my intellect: true wit.' But to-night she has soared into a region whither I may not follow her, save with the reverential eyes of an earth-bound loiterer; she has been accepted among the musical elect, and henceforward I can only offer my homage from below. Tho' such as it is—the tribute of enchanted ignorance—it is hers most heartily; and I ask you all to join with me in drinking the health of the 'Woman who has won!'"

"The woman who has won!" repeated Thorndyke, significantly, in Kathleen's ear. He had crossed over for the first time to be near her, and his gaze was radiant.

"Now, why couldn't I say some of those fine-sounding things?" poor Colin was grumbling inwardly, as he saw Kathleeen break into well-pleased smiles and bend blushing in the direction of her extoller. "Old Malvolio has no business to take this on himself, considering he's no more musical sense than a turnip. That's my trouble, after all. I can't keep up with the phrase-makers in their eternal patter. And that man she is talking to her now! How am I to tell Morry or her father the way I heard him speak of her a while ago? How did he get here, anyway? Anybody can get in with Kathleen better than I, it seems. If she'd give me only one of the sweet looks she wastes upon all these literary freaks"—such, we grieve to say, was the classification made by Mr. Mackintosh of the rank and file of the Blairs' associates—"I'd—"

His meditations were cut short by Kathleen herself, who, supple as a snake, had glided unnoticed to his elbow.

"You are the only one among us who has a long face," she said to him, softly, while across and around the table now resounded a fusillade of merry sayings and laughter. "Is it because you disapprove of my playing in public?"

"Disapprove of you? Oh! good gracious, no!" he answered, incoherently. "I am proud to the core of my heart. But that doesn't mean I like to think of you on a platform. It makes me wretched, and that's the honest truth. You ought to be shut in from vulgar gazers in a little world of your own; and the question of dirty money oughtn't to enter into your art."

"Perhaps not," said the more practical Kathleen; "but, after all, 'dirty money' puts the hall-mark upon accomplishment. And as to the vulgar gazers and hearers, they light the torch of genius. When I was last at the opera, in those good seats in the parquet Mr. Toner sent papa, I watched the artists closely, and saw that every one of them was working with all his or her might to do the best possible; and whenever there came a burst of real applause—not that little rainfall of claps one hears from the gallery alone, but the kind that comes, quick as near-by thunder after lightning, from the body of the house—the ease and spontaneity of the performance was increased. The very muscles of their bodies seem to feel the tension, and their faces to grow more luminous."

"That may be true," said poor Colin, who was again out of his depth; "but somehow, I don't fancy you among them. I had rather see you in the boxes with those nice girls who sit up by their mammas, and have fellows dropping in to call on them."

"Please don't!" cried she, with unaffected earnestness. "I can't imagine any life that would suit me less than theirs. Sometimes, on a winter's night when daddy and I hurry by them in the lobby, on our way to catch a cable car to get home in, I think maybe I might enjoy wearing one of their long fluffy white wraps like plumage—that look like seraphs' overcoats—and having a footman in a fur cape to call my carriage. But really, I don't want riches or fashion; I want opportunity only, and travel, and all the music I can get, and flowers like those orchids, and a new evening frock—and such nice things as Mr. Thorndyke has been saying to me about my touch, and—and to see my parents take a little rest from work. But that's what I talk about to Morry, not to you. When his ship and mine come in, you'll see what we shall do with our cargoes."

Thus it was always. While she filled every chink and cranny of Colin's dreams of the future, he had no part in hers. Swallowing his pain, he tried to find something to say to her about his pleasure in her success. He dared not venture in this place to criticise their new guest.

"Oh! thank you," she said, studying his appearance, apparently for the first time. "And to return the compliment, I ought to tell you that you look—really very nice."

"Morry put me up to it," he said, glowing with pleasure. "We had a council over my old evening rig that had been through three years of the University before it came to New York; and he decided I could no longer pass muster."

"Yes, I like you in these clothes," she said, critically. "But I think—though I'm not certain—your collar should not turn down so low—and I'm quite sure your hair is too long."

"Really?" he exclaimed, smiling ecstatically. It was so precious to have her speak to him in this proprietary way, even though he knew, too well, alas! that she was inspired by less than the interest of a sister. He would have been thankful, indeed, to have a part of Maurice's share in her regard.

"Yes, really," she said. "But for those minor points, I believe you are smart enough to appear in the gilded halls of Mrs. Beaumoris, where, by the way, I am to make my début on the twenty-fifth as a paid performer."

"You! oh, no!" he exclaimed, impetuously, his brown face reddening.

"And why not, pray?" she answered, proudly

237

resentful of his protest. "What has become of your theories about the dignity of honest toil?"

"It's not that—only—it is a chariot of fire that is coming to snatch you away from me," he said, simply, and in spite of herself Kathleen was touched.

Colin, seeing his advantage, tried to follow it up. But it is the misfortune of those in his peculiar state, that the very force of their desire to be agreeable to the beloved object defeats their chances of success. He could find nothing appropriate to say, and felt as he looked—large, lumbering, disconsolate.

No wonder Kathleen flitted away from him to laugh and chaff lightly with the others. Even little Catullus, with his poses and bushy hair and solemn fripperies, made the time pass for her more trippingly than did Morry's friend.

Terence, however, in his element as a host, presiding with rare grace and tact over their frugal feast, understood better than any one the art of amalgamating divers elements in a party. To their number was presently added Duval of the *Clarion*, who had just been writing his critique of the last new play at the —— Theater, that would help to form opinion on the subject next morning at many breakfast tables. Talk took itself wings, and soon was stirring with mirthful impulse.

Then Terence, who possessed a tenor voice that might have coined ducats for his family where his pen won them a bare livelihood, sang some of his Irish melodies—not Tom Moore's only, but Lover's, and the like. Gazing for an inspiration at his pretty Kathleen, he trolled out the delicious by-gone serenade that carried his wife back many a long year, and brought to her eyes the tears of tenderest sentiment.

"Oh! Molly Bawn, why leave me pining,
     All lonely waiting here for you, .
 When the stars above are brightly shining
     Because they've nothing else to do?

"The flowers late were open keeping,
     To try a rival blush with you;
 But their Mother Nature set them sleeping,
     With their rosy faces washed in dew.

"The wicked watch dog loud is growling;
     He takes me for a thief, you see;
 He knows I'd steal you, Molly darling,
     And then transported I should be.

"Oh! Molly Bawn, why leave me pining,
     All lonely waiting here for you,
 When the stars above are brightly shining,
     Because they've nothing else to do?"

Of all Mr. Blair's listeners the only one who wore an expression not in sympathy with the pretty tuneful old song was Catullus; and even he, sitting in a Yellow Book attitude, exhibited the grace of magnanimous forbearance. So rapt were the others in the charm of listening, they paid no heed to "a new step on the floor" of the adjoining room. It was a pattering little step, much as if a mouse was scuttling through the house; and at once the door opened, and in came a tiny, bright-eyed old lady, fully dressed and wide-awake, although her cap was a tiny bit askew.

"Granny!" cried her family in a voice.

"You didn't think, Terry, my boy, that I could stop upstairs in bed, and hear you sing the old songs down below," answered Granny, unabashed.

'You're like the 'good ould Oirish gintlemen, all of the oulden toime,' Granny," said Maurice, bringing forward her especial chair. "Don't you remember how he was supposed to be defunct, and his friends were 'waking' him, and the candles were lighted around his bed? The corpse stood all the rest, but when the whisky corks began to pop, he just sprang up and shouted, 'Whoop! Murther! d'ye think I'll be lying here dead, when such good stuff as that is flying around my head?'"

"For shame, saucy boy," said Granny, giving

her pet a little tap upon his hand that still clasped hers. "No supper, thanks; I couldn't survive it, really; and not a wee drop of the punch, even. Just go on with your nonsense, good people, and let me listen. But first come here, Kathleen, child, and tell me how you stood your trial."

"Let me settle your dear old cap, then," replied Kathleen, proceeding to put her offer into execution. "It's all right about me, Granny; I'm a gold mine, as you'll say when you know what Mrs. Beaumoris is going to pay me for playing at her party. And as to what Herr Levitsky said, that will keep for to-morrow. Now, papa, we want 'Widow Malone,' as only you can sing it."

"And afterward," added Thorndyke, with effusion uncommon in that measured personage, "Miss Blair will surely not refuse to give us a taste of her quality on the violin."

Therefore, in due course, Miss Blair, standing under the old clock, lifted her fiddle-bow, and lo! the air about them thrilled with exquisite sound. What she chose first to reproduce was the quaint German Christmas hymn, "Joseph, lieber, Joseph, mein," written by Calvisius five hundred years before. Then without warning she broke into Granny's favorite Irish jig, playing it with such resistless vim and merriment that every foot in the room began involuntarily to keep time, and every face wreathed itself into a smile. As quickly again the measure changed, and now Kathleen was back in Crichton's studio, and her hour of triumph was lived again.

"You are a real witch," said Colin, finding himself near her after this. "You have got all these people crazy about you. While you played, I was wondering if you'll ever be satisfied with any one man for an audience."

He turned, annoyed. There, behind him, stood Mr. Thorndyke, silent, inscrutable.

"Indeed, and I will!" Kathleen said, merrily.

"And what must he be or do to deserve it?"

"Be?" exclaimed the girl. "Like the donkey, all ears. And do? Give me a Stradivarius!"

A little later, when the company broke up and the guests went their several ways, Mackintosh, espying his forgotten flowers, had no longer the impulse to offer them to Kathleen. The events of the evening and the attentions of Thorndyke had made her recede further than ever from his reach.

"Will you ask your mother to have these lilies?" he said, awkwardly thrusting the box upon Maurice in the hall, and hurrying out of the house.

When Colin reached the spot he by courtesy
called home he let himself in with a latch-key at
a mean-looking door, and climbed three flights of
stairs to his den. This was not exactly the traditional hall-bedroom of the struggling clerk,
but a variant, in the shape of a middle room,
lighted and aired by a small skylight in the
roof only. In other respects it was as cheerless
as a ragged carpet, lame furniture, and mis-
matched crockery could make it; but Colin
thought little of personal comfort, and the gloom
of his meditation as he threw himself upon a
creaking chair beside his iron bed was not due
to the young man's meager surroundings. For
almost the first time in his life, he felt a sense
of impotency in meeting the future in fair fight;
and his ordinary trustful spirit rebelled against
thus leaving his affairs to "lie on the knees of
the gods!"

"Give her a Stradivarius!" he said aloud, bitterly. And, somehow, with the phrase mingled
a haunting thought of the man with the angel
face, who had in Colin's hearing spoken words
concerning Kathleen that were not in the least
angelic.

III

The words, "Give her a Stradivarius," had hardly been spoken aloud by young Mackintosh when he was surprised by a knocking upon the board partition dividing his attic room from the one adjoining it. After a pause, during which he listened, the knocking was renewed.

Colin, remembering that his neighbor was an infirm and melancholy looking old fellow, whom he sometimes met wearily climbing the stairs with a loaf of bread and a brown paper bag of comestibles hugged to his breast, fancied himself called upon for help. He had but just removed his coat and, putting it on, hastily ran out into the entry, and tapped at the door of the next room.

A feeble voice called to him to come in. The interior resembled Colin's own in lack of comfort. A gas-jet was burning, which revealed, lying dressed upon the bed close to the partition wall, the man he had often seen—gentle-faced, though hollow-eyed, and evidently racked by some chronic malady.

244

"I beg your pardon, sir," said Colin's neighbor, "but I must have been dreaming. I awoke suddenly, believing I heard some one distinctly say, 'Give her a Stradivarius!' And so I knocked on the wall, the way I used to call my nephew when he lived with me."

"I did say those words," answered Colin, blushing. "I was thinking aloud."

"I beg pardon again, sir," said the man, sitting up on the bed with an eager expression. "This is a coincidence I think you will agree is remarkable. I had fallen asleep thinking of a Stradivarius. I was dreaming of it. In fact, I rarely think of anything else, in these days. For to have owned something that in my present poverty would have been a little fortune, and to have had it stolen from me by my—Good God! I can't speak of him. It's too base for words. Mr. Mackintosh, I'm ashamed of myself. You see, I know your name. Mine is Rupert Thorndyke."

"That seems somehow familiar," said Colin, racking his brain to recall where he had heard the two names combined.

"No doubt, like most of us working folks, you read about the doings of the fine people who constitute high society in this town. Well, among them you have often seen that name. The other

Rupert Thorndyke is as young and pushing and successful as I am old and timid and collapsed. He is away up among the tiptops, Mr. Mackintosh—dines and wines with the millionaires, and gives parties at his own rooms. I eat bread and ham out of a paper bag upon yonder table, and am thankful when I can afford a bottle of beer or Rhine wine to wash it down. But he's of my own blood. My brother's son, and my only living relative—named for me, to my sorrow. When his father was in business with me in musical instruments at — Broadway I was the senior partner, and we prospered for many years. Then my brother got into speculations, and I had to make good the money he lost. Rupert, who was a clever dog, had been sent by me to the University. Well, my brother died of a broken heart; and Rupert came to live with me for a while. Got me to send him to Europe once or twice, which I could ill afford to do. He was such a handsome fellow, had such a winning way with him, one could refuse him nothing. Then some of his former classmates at college voted him into a fashionable club. I paid the entrance fee and dues, keeping my homely self out of sight of his grand companions. Mr. Mackintosh, you will wonder at my want of self-control. But you're a gentleman, and have got a heart, too—I can see it. I've often wanted to make your acquaintance."

"Go on, if it relieves you, Mr. Thorndyke," said the young man, dropping upon a chair beside the bed.

"Then you will honor me by drinking a glass of claret," said the other, arising with some difficulty from his recumbent position. "I am rather stiff with rheumatic pains, as you see. I lay down here before dinner to rest a while, and must have slept till now. Pray share my good luck. My employer—for I am serving where I once ruled, Mr. Mackintosh—gave me a bottle of Pontet Canet in honor of his birthday."

"I have just supped, thank you," said Colin, unwilling to hurt him by refusal. "But I'll have a glass of wine with you with pleasure."

The old man, shuffling about, produced glasses and a bottle, together with a Bologna sausage and some biscuits. As he sat munching and sipping opposite Colin at table, his dull eyes brightened with the feast.

"Good stuff, this," he went on. "I'll warrant the great Mr. Rupert Thorndyke has no more relish for his supper with the rich and exclusive Mrs. Beaumoris after the theater tonight! My employer gives me his morning paper when he has done with it, Mr. Mackintosh, and I bring it home, and under this gas-jet read the fashionable intelligence. I always know what's going on in society. Look at this old ledger; I have cut out and pasted in it all that is said about my namesake—where he goes, and what he does. Rupert is a musical virtuoso—hand in glove with all the artists, who sing and play at his rooms for nothing. The fine ladies attend, too, and admire the beautiful upholstery and decorations that I paid for when I was flush. Rupert has a collection of musical instruments, "small but unrivaled,' so the papers say. Mr. Mackintosh, I'd give a year of my life to look over that collection and make sure of my—my—lost Stradivarius."

"Do you mean to say—" began Colin, indignantly.

"When I failed in business I had saved that violin to be sold only in case of dire emergency. Rupert, better than another, knew its value. He always coveted it, but though I had squeezed myself dry to supply him, I would not give this up. For a long time, I should tell you, I kept on terms with my nephew. I never obtruded myself, but I saw him from time to time, taking a fool's pride in the grand gentleman I had created."

His head drooped forward. He seemed lost

in reverie. Colin, who had begun this adventure with indifference, felt his suspicions awaken and grow keen with the man's story.

"A pride I am afraid your nephew did not appreciate, Mr. Thorndyke," said the young man finally, to arouse him.

"Eh! Oh! of course not," exclaimed the instrument-maker, coming out of his trance. "I was thinking of what a handsome fellow Rupert is. His eyes are so blue, his smile so open, his manner so winning, no one under God's heaven would take him to be a—oh! *is* he that? Has my brother's boy fallen so low? He might have turned on the hand that fed and reared him; he might have shaken me off because I am poor and commonplace and rusty; but I can't believe— yet what must I believe? Listen, Mr. Mackintosh, to the proofs. After my failure, as I said, I had put away my precious Stradivarius in its case, in a trunk in the one room I kept—better than this, but still, one room only. I had to go over to Philadelphia, once, to see a man from whom I hoped to collect a few hundreds owing me. I came back rejoiced because I had got nearly the whole sum. The maid at the boarding-house said nobody had called or asked for me in my absence. I went straight to the trunk, and opened it to put away my cash. I found the violin-case empty—the treasure gone! Just as I was about to give the alarm to the house, I saw on the floor under the edge of the trunk, this—''

He took from his pocket an unset scarabeus, jade-green in hue, that might have been worn in a man's ring or pin.

"It was his. I had often seen him wear it in a scarf. He had showed it to me on his first return from Cairo. How could I alarm the boarding-house, or set the police upon the track of Rupert? Rupert a th— Oh, no! I won't say the word! Not till it's proved will I call him so. I found traces of wax on my latch-key of the house door, that I had been in the habit of throwing, with my other keys, on the dressing-table every night. Rupert had recently sent a man there with a note enclosing me a present of twenty-five dollars. While I wrote the answer the man must have taken the impression of my keys. Mr. Mackintosh, I had mistrusted that gift of money, though I kept it to pay my way to Philadelphia, and my board. Although I had given Rupert all, it was the first he had given me. I returned it to him the day after my discovery of the loss, with two lines, "Take your money, and give me back my Stradivarius." He answered in such a brutal tone it makes me

sick to think of it, disclaiming all knowledge of
my Stradivarius. I burnt his letter, but these
words are sunk into my heart, 'From this time
forth I refuse to see or to speak to one who has
done me this foul wrong.' That was two years
ago, Mr. Mackintosh—two years ago. I have
not prospered since; I am living on a pittance
of pay because the times are hard, and my employer has nothing like the business *we* used to
have. Are you cold, sir? If so, I can light the
gas-stove. I keep it for *very* cold weather generally. My nephew, as I said, has gone to a
play to-night, to see Sara Bernhardt, with a party
invited by Mrs. Beaumoris. His friends are
very exclusive, and he is a great favorite—or
perhaps it was last night he went to the theater;
I am losing my memory, you see."

"How does he continue to cut such a dash
without fortune?" asked Colin, anxious to satisfy
himself without exciting the poor old fellow's
suspicion.

"Nobody knows exactly. He was always
lucky in speculation, and very daring. I gave
him money to start with—all I could spare—and
he went on and on. Yes, he must have a good
purse to live as he does. I don't envy Rupert;
but oh! if I had the courage to go to-night and
try to get into his rooms—to say I am his uncle

and could wait till he came in—and then search there, and find out—''

"Perhaps he has sold the Stradivarius," said Colin.

"Oh, don't say that, Mr. Mackintosh. I hope against hope that he's keeping it as the gem of his collection—that I may one day look at it again. I'd know it in a hundred. There is a tiny vein of color in the wood, that looks like a hand with an outstretched finger, on the right side, near the bridge of the instrument. Enough for any one—for you, for instance, who know nothing of violins, to identify it by. But I'd know my beauty, as far as I could see her!''

As he filled a cracked glass with grape-juice for the third time and tossed it off, Colin saw that unusual treat had affected his poor old brain.

"*In vino veritas*, Mr. Mackintosh," he resumed, smiling wistfully. "I've told you my story as it hasn't passed my lips since I got my death wound. You go into society, don't you? I judge from this," touching the sleeve of Colin's evening coat.

"To a very limited degree," said Mackintosh, feeling much abashed.

"Because, I thought if you do, it might come in your way to help me." But in the act of making this suggestion the instrument-maker forgot what he had begun to say. He wandered, grew drowsy; and Colin, soon aiding him to bed, left him there sound asleep.

The pathos of this incident dwelt with Mackintosh for days. He longed to tell Kathleen, whose interest, he knew, would be keenly aroused in view of the object of the old artisan's mania. But in one way or another Colin failed to see any of the Blair family. He continued to meet Thorndyke on the stairs, and to exchange greetings with him. There was, however, no repetition of the first attempt at confidence. Thorndyke, as if aware that he had betrayed too much, looked shy of further converse with his stalwart and friendly young neighbor. Colin had almost begun to think the whole story a dream.

At last, when the need to look upon Kathleen's bright face became overpowering, Colin turned, late one afternoon, through a softly falling veil of snow in the direction of the Blairs' house. As he shook off the feathered flakes upon their door mat, he pleased himself by believing he would be asked to walk at once into the cosy intimacy of the family room, where at that hour Kathleen and her mother were wont to meet for tea.

Kathleen would be wearing her gown of brown

serge, with the slashes of crimson, that so well became her glowing brunette beauty—looking like the genius of home! Mrs. Blair would put away her galley slips and blue pencil, and come over to the tea-table beside the coal fire. Both of these gentle creatures would turn upon him the gaze of friendliest interest.

Colin's gateway of hope, in the shape of Mr. Blair's front door, moved inward. Behind it stood an elderly woman, endeavoring to dry her parboiled hands upon a checked apron before receiving the visitor's card between thumb and finger.

"Yes, sir, gone out; both Miss Kathleen and the madam," she said, with bursting pride. "It was in a cab that I fetched meself from the stable. Some kind of a grand music party, where our young lady was goin' to play, sir; and they'd not be out of it till after six. No. 6— Fifth Avenue, sir, they told the coachman. Perhaps you'd be knowin' the house, Mr. Mackintosh?"

Colin, blessing his stupidity in forgetting that this was Kathleen's important twenty-fifth, retraced his steps. Down fell his air-castle of a quiet hour with her. Vanished his fond imagining of some token from her of sweet half-hidden regret that they had been so long apart. With

cruel clearness of sight he beheld the true ambition of her life. By the time he should have
taken a slow step higher in his profession, Kathleen would have soared into an empyrean,
whither he could not follow. Henceforward a
fret and fever for public approbation would possess her young being; she would be forever
unfitted to plod through life at a poor man's
side—and, spite of his great love, Colin had no
mind to be the appendage of a successful public
favorite.

Doggedly, obstinately, the young fellow
tramped far uptown, welcoming the sting of wind
and snow in his face. Near the confines of
the Park he found himself, his bare hands in the
pockets of his overcoat, his face reddened with
cold, his jaw set, his eyes heavy, brought to a
halt before the house indicated to him by the
Blair's voluble maid.

There could be no doubt that a festivity was
in progress behind the brick and marble front
here presented to the avenue. Over a carpet
running out to the curbstone, guests were passing
to and from their carriages, beneath the shelter
of an awning lighted by pendent lanterns. Spite
of the snow, the aperture on either side the
tunnel of striped canvas was blocked, not only
by footmen comfortably humped in mountains

of black fur, but by the lookers-on, who seem to be never tired of this common phase of a city's pleasuring.

Colin, on the outer edge of one flank of the vagrant army, stood for a while, governed by some impulse he could not have explained. Among his comrades were one or two women and children, miserably clad, content to stand gaping at the show. Colin, to all appearance one of their class, excited no surprise, except that a tawdry girl wearing an old feather boa coquettishly around her throat asked him with some vexation not to go crowding other folks out of the places they had got before he came.

A lady effecting her exit from the house, was met by a young man who had just jumped out of a hansom, whom she greeted in accents maternally affectionate.

"So late, Mr. Thorndyke?" she said, in staccato reproach. "It's almost over now, and Levitsky will play no more. But Anatolia is just about to sing her last. Nothing would tempt me to leave, but that Nita, poor girl, is at home with a bad throat."

"It's a success, then?" said (ignoring Nita) the young man, at whom Colin Mackintosh gazed eagerly, seeking to be convinced of his identity with the thief of the Stradivarius.

He was handsome, golden-haired, open-faced, smiling. What a brave nephew for the old neighbor on the attic landing! But Colin did not know his Christian name, and that—

"Ha, Rupert," said a man, coming out. "Why are you behind time? There's a new girl playing on the violin that I know will please your fastidious fancy."

The lady's trim little brougham now stopping the way, the two young men aided her footman to introduce her goodly bulk within its open door. At this achievement, the group around the awning uttered an "A—a—h!" of satisfaction, and the carriage drove away.

"Any new violinist that is worth the asking you may count upon at my party on Wednesday night," said Thorndyke, carelessly. "And as I know the young person in question fairly well, I have little doubt of getting her to do what I wish. If you are *épris*, Clarkson, drop in and I'll give you a chance at her."

"All right, old chap, good-by."

As the two men separated, Colin clenched his fists.

None too soon for Kathleen's eager ambition had arrived the day of her appearance before an audience that would make or mar her hope of establishing herself as a performer. at semi-private concerts.

Punctual to the hour appointed by her patroness, the rusty cab, that in the eyes of the Blairs' maid servant had conferred style upon their dwelling by pulling up in front of it, had deposited at the Beaumoris portal the young violinist and her mother.

In a wide hall, beneath orange trees ranged against tapestries of great age and fabulous value, they were received by two automata in claret and silver livery, whose mission on gala days it was to forever point out to guests the way toward distant cloak-rooms. The fiddle-case, no less than the hesitating manner of their entry, betraying our ladies to these potentates, they were hurried with scant courtesy upstairs, and bidden to wait in the morning-room until the pleasure of the mistress concerning them should be ascertained.

Kathleen saw the flush on her mother's cheek at the moment when Molly caught the gleam in her child's eye.

"Don't mind, darling."

"It's a mistake, of course, dearest," were spoken simultaneously. Thereupon the two grasped hands for a little reassuring squeeze, and looked around them comforted.

Neither had seen anything comparable to this boudoir, its fantastic furnishings gathered from every quarter of the globe, its floor strewn with skins and rugs soft as velvet, its litter of costly curios, and cushions heaped upon gilded couches. Kathleen, getting up to pace the room with a free, impatient step, paused oftenest before the clusters of long-stemmed roses that hung their royal heads over the rim of tall crystal vases, and the gems of pictures upon the satin background of the walls. Then standing amazed by the writing-table, with its fittings and toys of beaten silver, she whispered, merrily:

"What a contrast to our war-worn old writing things at home. Upon this blotter one could only write invitations to a Vere de Vere."

She was interrupted by a Frenchwoman, whose entry, with the glib assurance that Madame would see them shortly, conveyed more of comradeship than of respect.

There was a long wait. Kathleen, wearied of her splendid prison, employed her time by falling upon a novel, of whose contents she possessed herself after the rapid fashion of the reader accustomed to absorb new books.

Mrs. Blair took up no volume. In silence she sat thinking of the days when she and Lottie Earl, now the owner of this stately domicile, had been schoolmates and bosom friends. To shut her eyes to the Beaumoris luxury was to conjure up Lottie's early home in Clinton Place, whither Molly had often repaired by invitation to spend Saturdays. The sad-colored walls hung with dreary landscapes in oil, upon which no eye was ever seen to cast a fleeting glance; the carpet and curtains flowered garishly, the basement dining-room, the little girls exchanging vows of friendship!

A more tender memory was that of the day when Lottie's mother had died. Was it not Molly for whom they had sent to soothe and console the terrified child? Molly's faithful breast upon which Lottie that night had sobbed herself to sleep?

The door again opened. This time it was Mrs. Beaumoris in person, attired for the reception of her guests—Mrs. Beaumoris, perplexed, annoyed, an open letter in her hand. It was an easier matter for this lady to recognize fresh, bright-eyed Molly Christian, who, under the impulse of fond retrospect, now sprang up to greet her, than for Molly to identify her old playmate in this faded woman, with the pale hair elaborately crimped, the cold, restless blue eyes—the prim, unsmiling mouth!

Mrs. Blair's affectionate words died upon her

lips. She faltered, blushed, and drew back with a pang at the plain indication that her surprise was as unwelcome as it was ill-timed.

"You—you—are Miss Blair's mother?" said Mrs. Beaumoris, in tones she could not make other than thin and chill. "Why was I not told of this before?"

"Because—because," began Molly, and emotion overpowered her, cutting short her speech.

"My mother thought it could naturally make no difference whose child you had hired to play before your guests," said Kathleen, sweeping grandly into the breach. "But we are quite ready to go away now, if the arrangement does not please you."

"Of course not," exclaimed their hostess, recovering herself. "You will excuse me if I am a little upset, when I tell you that not fifteen minutes ago I received this letter from Madame Claudia's manager, saying the tiresome creature has a cold and can't sing this afternoon. All I could do was to send off my maid in a cab, offering Claudia's terms to Anatolia, who'll come, I'm pretty sure, if for nothing but a chance to supplant Claudia. Anatolia can't stand being last year's favorite, and really she sang adorably in Faust last week, when Claudia was ill, don't you think so—or did you not chance to hear her? If she comes, she'll be here for the end of the first half of the programme. Your daughter will play just before her—and will no doubt have encores. Levitsky says everything that is nice of you, Miss—er—you have no professional name, I believe?''

"My name is Kathleen Blair," said the girl, carrying her head high. Into her heart, for the first time in her life, entered the wandering demon of revenge. She longed to be in a position to return impertinence!

Kathleen's second number upon the programme of Mrs. Beaumoris's concert left no doubt of her success. Levitsky himself had conducted her before the audience. Madame Anatolia had coquettishly (in view of the audience) presented the girl with her corsage bouquet of violets. As Kathleen retired again into the little room serving as a harbor for the performers, the musical Miss Beaumoris (who kept outsiders from intruding there), looking very sour, asked Miss Blair to allow Mr. Rupert Thorndyke to compliment her upon her achievement.

Kathleen possessed just enough of the spice of Mother Eve to see that this courtesy on the part of Miss Beaumoris had been wrung from her by the newcomer. Madame Anatolia, whom Mr. Thorndyke saluted with an air of cordial intimacy, leaned over and whispered in the young girl's ear:

"Take care how you enjoy the dangerous delight of his company in *this* house. They consider him their own particular property."

Molly Blair, standing guard over her beautiful and successful child, could not understand the reckless toss of Kathleen's head, the defiance of her curled lip.

"That lends zest!" Kathleen answered to Anatolia, who smiled. The prima donna, knowing the world as she did, had no objection to enjoy a small comedy behind the scenes. Nor was she disappointed. Rupert Thorndyke, with an air of entire unconsciousness, refrained from again turning toward the musical Miss Beaumoris. With his handsome head bent over the newly risen star, he exerted all his powers of fascination. He was no longer the cool, indifferent person who had dropped in at the Blair's little supper. Kathleen, excited, inclined to accept him at his face value as a favored frequenter of the Beaumoris's house, and finding herself not a little under the spell of his charm of manner and sympathy of taste, enjoyed retaining him. Until the time Mrs. and Miss Blair left the Beaumoris's house he was in close attendance at their side. And when they parted he had obtained Mrs.

Blair's rather dazzled permission to call upon them the next day.

Thorndyke, meaning to put these ladies in their carriage, was recalled on the portal by the imperious Miss Beaumoris, who had, she said, to consult him about a protégé of hers she desired to launch at his musicale on Wednesday.

"Until to-morrow, then," said Rupert Thorndyke, regretfully turning back.

"Mother, he is absolutely beautiful!" said Kathleen, with a girl's ecstasy, as they went down to stand on the sodden carpet waiting for their cab to come up. "I think he must be some prince in disguise, or something! Such a noble air, such aristocratic features! And better than all, mummy dearest, he has confided to me that he gives music parties at his rooms, and we're asked to the next one, on Wednesday."

"I suppose it is all right," said Molly. "Or, of course, the Beaumorises would not be having him."

"They can't always get him, as you saw," said Kathleen, laughing. "I hope it was not wicked to be as glad as I was when I saw their two cross faces while he talked so long to me. But never mind the man, mother. There is a joy still greater in store for me. He says if I'll play for him on Wednesday, I may handle his Stradivarius!"

The cab that had brought Miss Blair to the scene of her triumphs was not forthcoming. The hoarse calls for it up and down the line were unavailing.

"It's but a step to the street-car, mother, if we run for it," cried Kathleen, gayly, peering into the half-darkness at the open side of the awning.

"I will take you home, if you don't mind," said a voice out of the crowd, and Colin edged his way toward them!

Colin was cold and out of humor. But he had lingered on, and this was his reward.

"How delightful to see you!" exclaimed his lady-love, heartily, and was indorsed by her mamma. "So strange you should be passing just at this minute! It will be ever so much nicer having you, of course. Now let us run, and jam ourselves into the next car."

Mrs. Blair being seated with the violin-case on her lap, the two young people stood side by side in the crowded aisle of a Madison Avenue car going downtown. Colin heard from his eager comrade the full account of her exhilarating afternoon. It made him sad, even while his generous heart rejoiced in her rejoicing, to see that she was already embarked with sails filled and pennons flying upon the broad sea that would separate them. And he wondered she said nothing about the person whose name excited his keenest curiosity.

Perhaps Kathleen felt guilty of having hailed rather too gladly Mr. Rupert Thorndyke's distinguished homage. But even Madame Anatolia had told her that his verdict was of importance in the musical world.

"We all bow to him," had said the good-natured donna; "and he is badly spoiled, of course. Don't let your feelings get involved, like that poor, ugly Miss Beaumoris. Thorndyke is a mystery—and, I'm afraid, *volage!*"

Kathleen had laughed! She had no fear for herself.

"And you are to keep on with this kind of thing?" now said Colin, discontentedly.

"Of course!" exclaimed she. "Two ladies have already booked my humble services; although one of them *did* say, in excuse for herself, that anything Mrs. Beaumoris started is sure to run on for a while."

"I shall never hear you perform," he went on. "So I'll try to forget it. If I had my way, I'd carry you off to a cloud-castle and keep you shut in from all these insolent people."

"But you can't, Master Colin, so be satisfied,"

said she, coloring a little at the fervor he could
not exclude from his tones. "And as to hearing me, you shall have an opportunity without
delay. Let us see if you are so eager to accept
it."

"I will go wherever you bid me," he replied,
more and more under the charm of her close
vicinity.

"Promise."

"I promise."

"How one's eloquence is jolted out of one by
this!" she said, as they swung around the curve
into the tunnel. "Well, here is your chance.
Next week we are invited to a very exclusive
musicale. Levitsky's to be there, and Anatolia—
and I'm to play (think of it, Colin!) on a Stradivarius! Wait, don't interrupt me. We were
asked to bring my father, or brother, as our
escort, and neither papa, nor Morry can get off,
I know. Papa has a club meeting, and Morry's
slaving, day and night, to finish ——'s illustrations. So, if you'll take us to the party, we'll
be only too much obliged."

"I will, of course. But tell me—it is a matter
of the deepest interest—who is to furnish your
Stradivarius?"

"It belongs to the gentleman who is to give
the party, and Madame Anatolia says his rooms

and collection of musical instruments are 'things to be seen.' He is one of the favorites of fortune, and is coming to call on us in form to-morrow—and his name is—Rupert Thorndyke!''

"I thought so," said Colin, turning pale with excitement, and perhaps a little jealousy.

"What, you, too, know about the wonderful Mr. Thorndyke? Oh! but, of course, I remember, you met him at supper at our house when he brought me those white orchids, and you gave mamma some lilies. Don't you think his face is like one of the angels in the photograph over papa's chair in the library? Now, don't laugh— it is, exactly. Mr. Thorndyke isn't in the least my idea of a man of fashion. He is almost artless—and his eyes are *so* blue. Colin, what in the world is the matter with you?"

"I do know something of your Mr. Rupert Thorndyke," said the young man, his face darkening. "But I shan't tell you yet. It is borne in upon me that a better occasion will come. And if you really accept my escort, I shall accompany you with pleasure to this gentleman's party. A poor outsider, more or less, cannot spoil his harmonious entertainment."

Kathleen, wondering at all this, reached home, the ladies bidding Colin good-by upon their doorstep. That evening, when Malvolio dropped in to see Terence Blair, the news of Kathleen's advance up the ladder of fame was communicated to him.

"Sure and Kathleen's the boldest little girl," commented Granny. "It's my belief she'd have no fear to be called on to play before the President himself."

"I know little about Rupert Thorndyke," said Terence; "but there's no doubt he will have only the best talent in his sling. But you, Malvolio, who know everything—"

"Excepting the reason for Catullus Clarke," interpolated the art critic.

"—should be able to define for us the place of our new patron in the arts."

Malvolio shrugged, tossing his snaky locks to one side of his high, white forehead.

"Rupert Thorndyke's secret will never be fathomed until they dissect him," he said; "and then in the core of his heart will be found the one word 'Self.' He is a monumental egoist, in the guise of a seraph. He is brilliant and treacherous, unstable as water, holding no convictions long enough to make anything he says or does of lasting value. I am certain that he is half-educated, half-baked in all respects. I believe most of his 'experiences' of life to be clever adaptations from things other people have done, or told, or printed. But he is vastly good company, and I'd be deuced glad if he were coming to dine with me to-morrow. As to his status, he is apparently well off—has one foot in Bohemia, the other in society—and comes from nobody knows where. Lastly, we are informed that he might marry the oldest Miss Beaumoris, and does not aspire to do so!"

The blushes dyed Kathleen's cheeks at the confirmation of Colin's warning.

"Then you think, Mr. Malvolio, our girl had better not be seen at his party?" said Mrs. Blair, anxiously.

"My *dear* madame! On the contrary. I should like amazingly to be seen there myself. It is sure to be a rare treat to eye and ear. The women will be of the highest world only. The men judiciously combined. But I have always had an idea that Thorndyke will some day come a cropper. I feel like that fellow that followed the menagerie around in order to be there the day the lion-tamer should get eaten by the lions. The day the accident occurred was the one he was kept away. I have a conviction I shan't see Thorndyke's discomfiture—but I could wish that, to round out my theory of him, the fates might accord to me this privilege."

Kathleen, who would not have admitted to her mother even, the thrill of excitement she had been in since receiving the first fruits of Thorndyke's homage, went to bed that night, feeling chastened in her pride. With her last waking thoughts of the irresistible Thorndyke, blended the image of loyal Colin, whom, after consultation with their maid-servant, she now knew to have been waiting outside Mrs. Beaumoris's awning for her in the falling snow.

Molly Blair, too, following a long talk with her husband, that freed her fond heart of its weight of pride in and anxiety for Kathleen, went to sleep happy. With so many loving souls around her, Terence had said, Kathleen would be well guarded, and such a fine nature as their girl's was not to be spoiled in an hour or a year by flattery. And Molly's last thoughts that night were of pity for poor Lottie Beaumoris. The afternoon of sitting out the concert, listening to the chatter of Lottie's friends, had thrown broad light upon a career the newspapers had made to seem so dazzling. Lottie, weighed down with petty cares, a target for petty malice, was in her fine home not so well off as Molly in her little threadbare house, full to the eaves with ardent workers, living for each other and

for the best that was in them. Kathleen's
début had taught her mother this!

Carefully assuming his recently acquired evening clothes, and taking heed, we may be sure, of
the hints dropped by Kathleen on the occasion
of his former appearance in this conventional
attire, Mr. Colin Mackintosh stood prepared for
what to him was to be a great occasion.

Before setting out to the Blairs' house he went
to his neighbor's door and knocked. He knew
that he should find Mr. Thorndyke sitting doubled
up over his newspaper, under the gas-jet; but
to-night the old man's face looked more pinched
and wan than usual, his breath came shorter,
the newspaper lay unread across his kneés.

"I'm afraid you're ill," said Colin, kindly.

Hardly a day had passed since their first talk
that he had not extended to the friendless old
fellow some word or look of sympathy; and
Thorndyke, although Colin did not know it, had
conceived for him in turn an almost paternal
tenderness. In the utter loneliness of his life
the instrument-maker yearned for something to
link him with the world of everyday affection.
Colin's active step upon the stairs had come to
be music to his ear—Colin's greeting a solace
eagerly awaited.

"Not ill, my dear boy; only a little down to-night. I begin to feel the climb up these long flights. And so you are going off into some gay scene, where people will be chatting and laughing? I don't envy you, for it's getting on to ten o'clock, and after that hour I can hardly keep awake in these days. There's a long paragraph—nearly half a column—in the paper about an affair that is to occur in my nephew's rooms to-night. I think I could tell you everybody that's expected there. There's a young violinist—a Miss Blair—who has made a hit recently—and some famous professionals. Mr. Mackintosh, I ought to tell you, too, that since I let out that secret that's corroding me I have felt much ashamed. There was only this excuse for it—a very little drink affects me, and I had already had a glass of beer on my way home. The claret finished me. It did not confuse my brain, but just loosed my tongue. What I told you was true, but it should have gone with me to my grave."

"You need never fear my making use of it unfairly," said Colin, pityingly. The meek submission of the man was sadder than his outburst of wrath had been.

"I know I can trust you. I wish it were in my power to do something for you, Mr. Mackintosh.

If I die soon, you will have given me the last gleams of pleasure in a disappointed life. I wish I could help you in return."

"You can to-night," said Colin; "if you do not mind lending me, for a purpose of my own, the fine scarabeus you showed me. It shall be returned to you without fail to-morrow."

"Willingly, dear boy, willingly," said the old man, fumbling in his waistcoat pocket and bringing out the sacred beetle wrapped in a bit of tissue paper. "When I die I should like you to have this to keep, and any other little thing I have. There are a few good books, and—"

"My dear friend, you depress me," said Colin, taking the scarabeus, and shaking hands with the lender.

"Do I? It never occurs to me to think of my death as *sad*," said Thorndyke, simply.

"Suppose," said Colin, abruptly, "you had to wish for the thing that would please you most—what would it be?"

"A sight of my Stradivarius!" exclaimed the instrument-maker, his dull eye kindling with fond hope. "Mr. Mackintosh, something in your face—it can't be you have heard—no, I'm a madman to dream of it—but it almost looked for a minute as if you have good news."

"I may be wrong, and I may be disappointed,"

said Mackintosh, with an air of quiet conviction, nevertheless. "But I have an idea I'm on the track of your lost treasure. If I succeed in tracing it, I shall be more than glad. If I fail, you will be no worse off than before. Good night. Sleep well, and awake in better heart for the morrow. But before I go,—upon second thoughts,—I wish you would give me a written order for your Stradivarius."

After Colin left his room old Thorndyke abandoned himself to almost childish glee. Next, for a while, he paced the floor, then, sinking fatigued into his chair, meditated long.

It was twelve o'clock when he started up again, and taking the pencil with which he had scrawled and signed the order Colin desired, wrote some lines upon a paper torn from a memorandum book. Putting these upon the table, old Rupert Thorndyke went peacefully to bed.

At the same moment Rupert Thorndyke the younger was presiding over the entertainment at his rooms, for which fine ladies had been for some time struggling to get cards of invitation. The host's vogue, grace, and tact had been at no time more conspicuous. The affair, pronounced the best of its kind, was about to pass into the chronicle of jaded pleasure-seekers as an eminent success. The turn of Kathleen, who had played once upon her own violin, had now come around again upon the programme. Mr. Malvolio—who, after all, *was* there—had just sauntered up to whisper in her ear:

"They say he is going to let you try his Stradivarius. The rest of the women are green with jealousy at this mark of favor. No one has touched it heretofore."

"If Mrs. Blair will allow her daughter to come with me into the little room where I keep my treasure—" Thorndyke was saying to her mother, who, with Colin behind her, stood guard over her young violinist.

"Certainly. Go with her, Colin, please, and see that her head is not quite turned by these honors," said the unconscious Molly.

Colin needed no further impetus. In spite of a cloud passing over the face of their handsome host, the stalwart fellow placed himself at Kathleen's side and accompanied them.

A room of small dimensions, but with solid doors, bolted as well as locked. On the walls, in glass cases with a background of crimson velvet, a small but exquisite assemblage of what might be called the bric-à-brac of musical instruments. Violins were there, but Colin's eye sought in vain for one bearing the mark of a tiny hand with an outstretched finger.

"What a delightful nook!" cried Kathleen. "How I wish there were time to look over its wonders leisurely."

"Some day—any day that you so ordain," said the virtuoso. "I and mine are at your command always."

Colin, seeing Thorndyke's face transfigured with delight in the girl's youth and beauty, raged inwardly. He recalled the value he had heard him put upon all women, Kathleen in particular. Strong as a lion to defend her, it was hard for the young fellow to now contain himself until he had wrought out his plan to avenge the sins of this Rupert Thorndyke against the one he had left in a shabby tenement.

He had no idea how he meant to bring about the conviction of this man's wrong-doing, or to seek for the restoration of the other's stolen property. But whatever he did, Colin meant that it should be short, sharp, and decisive!

At last chance favored him. His heart beat hard as he followed Kathleen and Thorndyke from object to object of the priceless array.

"I fear we should not keep all those people waiting for us longer—" said the host finally.

"And I am palpitating with impatience to see your chief treasure," cried Kathleen.

"I have made a little shrine for it," went on

Thorndyke, stooping to unlock a cupboard in the wall. A second inner door of polished mahogany yielded to a key carried on the owner's person. Within an air-tight receptacle lay a violin-case, covered with rare leather fantastically wrought in gold.

"Take and open it," said Thorndyke, conveying this to a nest in Kathleen's soft bare arms. "You are the first woman that I have entrusted with my beauty."

"My beauty!" Old Thorndyke's very phrase! Colin, the blood rushing to his brain with excitement and indignation, looked on eagerly as the instrument was taken from its case. There, in the exact spot indicated by its rightful owner, was a tiny shadow in the wood resembling a hand with an outstretched finger!

"The desire of my life is accomplished," said Kathleen, lifting the violin to her shoulder and letting the bow glide over the strings.

The sound that answered was like the wail of a reproach.

"It has been waiting all this time for you!" said Thorndyke, with tender emphasis, regardless of their hearer. He, like Kathleen, seemed to be under a sort of spell.

"Since when, may I ask?" interrupted Colin, quietly.

Thorndyke turned and looked at him in cold distaste.

"Since the creation of the instrument, no doubt. Certainly since it came to me by inheritance."

"By inheritance?" said the younger man, with deliberate doubt in his intonation. "I think, Mr. Thorndyke, that your uncle, who bears the same name as yourself, would give a different version of the way you acquired this costly possession."

Thorndyke started violently.

"Do you mean to insult me?" he said in almost a whisper, guilt written in his face.

Kathleen, spell-bound by Colin's stern looks, held the violin breathlessly.

"I mean, Mr. Thorndyke, to make absolutely no fuss in this very unpleasant matter. But I mean also to make it perfectly plain to you that I know all about this Stradivarius with the mark of a hand pointing. I am informed when and how it was taken out of your uncle Thorndyke's trunk in his boarding-house. And if you will give it up to him quietly, I shall not say another word to any one concerning it."

"An ingenious method to possess yourself of a valuable piece of property," sneered Thorndyke, now livid with fear and rage.

"I have this to offer in exchange," said Colin, controlling himself perfectly, as he took out the scarabeus and held it, together with the old man's written order for the violin, for the inspection of the thief.

"My dear Colin," exclaimed Kathleen, greatly distressed and mortified at the scene. "You must take me back to my mother. I insist—"

"Just as soon as Mr. Thorndyke gives a definite answer to my proposition," said Colin, fearlessly.

Thorndyke breathed hard. His eyes flashed with a vengeful luster. He tried to speak, and could not. Then, looking furtively about the room, and seeming to grow smaller in the action, he took the Stradivarius from Kathleen, put it in an old and shabby case, and replacing the empty ornamental cover in the secret chamber, shut and locked this receptacle with elaboration. With a supreme effort, he recovered his usual manner.

"You will give this to my uncle, with my compliments," he said lightly, putting the precious violin in Colin's hands and reclaiming the scarabeus. "And you might say from me, that although I know the old boy is as mad as a March hare, I don't like to thwart his dear old fancy. I was about indeed, to inform him, through my lawyer, that a sum of money coming out of an old investment of his and my father's, has been divided, and his share placed to his credit in the —— bank. A thousand a year only, but enough to keep him in comfort in the lunatic asylum, where I feel sure he will bring up.''

Kathleen, although he had avoided and ignored her in the matter, had not waited for this ending. With crimson cheeks and in great agitation, she had slipped out to rejoin her mother. A few moments later heard their host, standing before his guests, offer a graceful explanation that the condition of his Stradivarius would prevent Miss Blair from to-night awakening its hidden melodies.

Colin, clasping the recovered treasure like the anchor of hope, was in the lobby awaiting the ladies when they presently hurried out. On the drive home he told them in simple but eloquent language the full history of his old neighbor and the stolen violin.

When he had finished, Molly was crying quietly. Kathleen's eyes flashed upon him such approval as he had never seen in them before.

''I could *love* you for what you've done for that poor old man, Colin,'' she cried, with Irish impulse, and stopped, blushing. ''But I don't understand why Thorndyke made such a poor fight."

"It was 'coward conscience,'" said Colin. "For if I read him right, he would cut off his right hand to avoid exposure or fiasco before such people as were there to-night."

"I could love you," rang joyously in Colin's ears as he ran up his own steps, carrying the violin. When he reached Thorndyke's room, late as it was, he could not resist trying to get speech with his friend. His light tap bringing no answer, he opened the door and went in. The light over the transom showed him the old man lying in his bed. Leaving the Stradivarius upon the table, Colin stole away.

The next day the people of the house found the old instrument-maker sitting in his chair, a happy smile upon his face, the violin clasped in his arms. He had been dead some hours, and on his table lay a penciled will, bequeathing all that he died possessed of, "without reserve," to his "beloved young friend, John Walter Mackintosh."

Thus, in due time, and to the enormous surprise of everybody concerned, Kathleen came into possession, not only of her coveted Stradivarius, but of a husband, with an income small but growing and sufficient to enable him to withdraw his wife from public appearance as a paid performer. Upon the authority of Mr. Rupert Thorndyke, who lives and flourishes like the green bay-tree, this is said to be a serious loss to the world of music, but Kathleen does not mind.

Malvolio still thinks the fall of Rupert Thorndyke is to come!

WANTED: A CHAPERON

WANTED: A CHAPERON

Gwendolyn West sat alone in profound meditation upon her future. She was the childless young widow of a naval officer, whom she had lost after six months of married life and two years of separation during his absence on official duty in foreign waters.

For three years she had mourned her lieutenant dutifully. No crêpe had ever exceeded Gwendolyn's in depth and plenitude. At the end of that time her free-spoken friend, Kate Payne—who had politely encouraged her illusion that the marriage was not a mistake—had told her she was tired of seeing her look like the German nursery picture of Slovenly Peter after he was fished out of the forbidden inkstand. Gwendolyn had laughed—and the deed was done. She had now emerged into alleviated grays and hopeful lilacs. Mrs. Payne, nodding approval, said she had never seen such a creature for making her clothes look stylish; and Gwendolyn, in return, owned that the materials cost nothing and were made up by a little woman "by the day."

"All the same, you look solvent, prosperous, up-to-date. What can woman ask more?" said Kate.

"Ask? My dear Kate, you have no idea how hard put to it I am to make ends meet. I am so poor it is a scandal. If my Aunt Althea had not invested her money in this flat, when the house was going up, and left it to me in her will, I should be living in one room of a boarding-house, with a folding-bed. As it is, I ought to let the flat and eke out my ridiculous little income with the proceeds. If I were abroad I might live on it almost in comfort."

"Nobody understands living abroad better than you do."

"Of course,. since from nineteen to twenty-four I knocked about there with Aunt Althea. But my difficulty, absurd though it may seem for a woman of almost thirty, is that I look hardly old enough to live as a solitary female in the places I know best on the other side. In New York I am panoplied with respectability."

"And boredom," supplemented the frank Mrs. Payne. "It is no fun to live here on the outside of things, where one has been used to

"MY DEAR KATE, YOU HAVE NO IDEA HOW HARD PUT
TO IT I AM TO MAKE ENDS MEET. I AM SO POOR IT IS A
SCANDAL."

the inside. The truth is, you ought to have had a girl—not a boy, who would have been a handful, and most probably a pickle—but a nice little golden-haired angel, with short skirts and long, black-stockinged legs, whom you would have made a vision of picturesqueness in dress."

"Let us talk of what I have," said Mrs. West, with a sigh.

"It has just occurred to me that you would make a capital chaperon for some breezy young woman of large means, scant culture, and consuming ambition to see the world. You have position, manners, morals beyond question, and would be a perfect teacher of how to dot one's i's in good society."

"What servitude!" exclaimed her friend, shuddering. "I detest breezy people who are uncertain of themselves. And there is nothing so delusive as temper. She might make my life a burden. How mortifying, too, to have to conduct her along the primrose paths of society in my own town! I should live over a volcano, never knowing when she would break forth."

"Take her traveling," went on Madame.

"That is better," said Gwendolyn. "But suppose she fell ill, or flirted, or defied me, away off there. She would be sure to do all three."

"I should do nothing without being well paid for it. With a full purse you can accomplish wonders."

"It would be such a relief to spend six months or a year free from looking over that hateful butcher's book. Although I know that I and my two maids eat nothing, our bills are awful, and I can't pretend to read butchers' handwriting, can you? '3 cucks, 0.90'; that's what I labored over for a whole morning, after I had ordered a miserable little cucumber to be cut up with my fish."

"I am afraid the queen of your kitchen is a wiser potentate than you credit her with being. But, my dear, I have an inspiration. Yesterday I got a circular from a new 'Bureau of Information Concerning Women's Needs.' It is intended to bring together refined and cultivated employers and employés, and to make a specialty of companions, chaperons, and governesses. Suppose I inquire—I know the woman at the head; she will take pains to oblige me—and see if she has any applications from young persons who have left school and desire to be 'finished' in the broadest sense—"

"Kate, Kate, you frighten me. You are such a steam engine in accomplishing what you set out to do I should be afraid to go out to walk this afternoon lest I should come in to find my treasure installed here in permanence.''

"You need not take her unless everything suits. I really believe such a girl would rouse you up, give you a new motive in life, and end by being a blessing in disguise—''

"Very much disguised," remarked Gwendolyn, ruefully.

"It is now late February. You could sail in March by the Southern route to Genoa, and spend the spring in Italy.''

Gwendolyn flushed and sat bolt upright. Her soul was pierced by the chant of nightingales in the Cascine woods; of the singers upon the star gondola by moonlight on the Grand Canal; of the Amalfi boatmen resting upon their oars! How well she would know where to go, and how to enjoy the best of everything. She had been starving for beauty for four years!

"Let me—let me have time to think," she said finally, with a sort of gasp.

"You poor victim, you have a most pathetic air," answered Mrs. Payne, getting up to go, and kissing her. "Of course, you must think over it. Let me know to-night; and to-morrow morning, bright and early, I will order the brougham and set forth upon my quest.''

A paid conductor and chaperon! Out of the

mists of recollection loomed up before Gwendolyn a time, when sitting with her aunt and her husband in the dining-room of a great hotel in Amsterdam, she had seen the entry of a hot, red-faced lady, preceding a string of girls of assorted sizes, and marshaling them at table. Their party was completed by one lean, henpecked little boy, presumably the conductor's son, obtaining free of expense educational glimpses into the vistas of old-world life.

From that day on Gwendolyn had continued to meet them during their stay—fortunately brief—in the great Dutch town. One of the girls had taken a fancy to Mrs. West, and whenever they came together in galleries and the like annexed herself to Gwendolyn, asking flat questions upon art, and detailing her grievances against the head of their party. Mrs. Batt was selfish; she had not fulfilled her promises to them; she hurried them through things they wanted to see; and lingered in places where the fare was good and cheap, in order to feed up her little boy.

And Mrs. Batt, in turn, running upon Gwendolyn in a corridor upstairs at their hotel, told her it was a dog's life she was leading, pulled around by these capricious girls, who didn't know what they wanted, and were forever having headaches and tiffs with each other, and taking offense about nothing, or else entering into conversations with strange men and thinking it clever. But for the advantage to her dear, fatherless child Mrs. Batt could wish herself back again in peace at New Corinth, Kansas, whence they had all set forth in May.

Recalling all this, Gwendolyn drew a long breath of dismay. Then the maid came in with a sheaf of household bills and the announcement that she and the cook had determined to leave when the month should be up. An organ-grinder in the street outside began to play:

"O! bella Napoli!
O! dolce Napoli!"

The sunshine that streamed through the panes of her south windows was full of suggestions of purple seas, overarched by an azure dome, beneath which roses bloomed along the shore, and jasmine and orange flowers distilled their richest perfume. Oh! to be in the South—far from the sound of trolley cars and all the tokens of a city's overcrowded life that, day or night, can never be hushed!

If she had something of her very own—some hearthside idol to go and come in her little home, she would be more than content to stay there.

Then Gwendolyn subjected herself to a secret crucial test. She opened a case of photographs—a receptacle made of old brocade, broidered with silver thread, that she had picked up in the Palais Royal in 1893—and extracted one of its portraits. This was an up-to-date affair, executed by a New York photographer of note. It represented a man of five-and-thirty, good looking, amiable, and weak.

She looked at it long and studiously. A line dashed off at her writing-table, a call for a messenger, a few hours' delay, and he would be with her. The very next day she might announce to all interested her engagement to marry Mr. Ernest Blythe. As Mrs. Blythe, provided she could maintain a sufficient interest in yachting and its devotees, no injunction would be laid upon her habits or inclination. Blythe was rich, easy-going to a ridiculous degree, as much in love with her as his capacity would admit, and was hers to take or leave.

But—Gwendolyn glanced up at an enlarged photograph of the late Lieutenant West, hanging in an ebony frame above that very writing-table, as if to control its output of chirographical amenities.

Her survey was not reassuring. "Oh! never, never again!" she murmured audibly. It is only once in a long while that women really speak to themselves aloud, and that is when they want a witness to some vow of a peculiarly binding character.

She took Mr. Blythe with hastening finger tips and drove him in at the very bottom of the pack. It would be a long time before she could take him out again.

Then something possessed her to go into a dark closet and hunt around upon its seldom-visited shelves to find a very old album of photographs, dating back before her travels in Europe with her nomadic Aunt Althea had weaned her from thoughts of home.

She was eighteen then, and was making a visit to the wife of a professor in a university town, where most of these treasures of pictorial art had been accumulated. What faded old things they were, chiefly of undergraduates wearing queer collars and scarfs, with coats that did not fit and hair that was much too long! She had some difficulty in finding the particular cabinet photograph she sought, but it appeared at last, looking straight at her with the fearless gaze of handsome eyes that had once held over hers unwonted power.

"Ten—more, nearly eleven—years ago," she mused. "He wore his hair like the sweep of a mahogany banister, poor dear; but *that was a man.*"

John Rufus Atwell was his rather uninteresting name. He was a young widower of twenty-six when he came back to take a post-graduate course at—— from his home in a Western town, where he had left his child with its mother's people. None of his surroundings or antecedents had appealed in the least to the æsthetic and superfine side of pretty Miss Gwendolyn. But he had fallen in love with her, just like half a dozen more of the youngsters. She had tried to treat him just like them—and had failed. He had given her a first lesson in virile resistance to the exactions of coquettish femininity.

They had parted, though she had always remembered him with something of tender regret. But still the thing would have been impossible—quite impossible! What had become of him since she had not the vaguest idea.

That evening a little note went to Mrs. Payne authorizing her to find out for her friend some one who wanted an unexceptionable chaperon.

Mrs. Payne had good reason to think that industrious intervention in a friend's affairs is sometimes approved by the Fates. The principal of the new "Bureau of Information Con-

cerning Women's Needs" expanded with satisfaction on hearing of her errand.

It so happened that one of the earliest applications that had come to them was from a family
in a Western State who desired to send their
daughter abroad under competent care. She had
looked into their references—although that was
scarcely needful when it was understood that the
father was the distinguished statesman, Honor-
able John Mordaunt, Senator from ——, whose
name was in every newspaper one took up.

Mrs. Payne, reserving her decision as to this
proof of infallible respectability, was pleased to
be interested in the matter. She next read Mr.
Mordaunt's letter to the principal, and put it
down even better pleased.

"That is nicely expressed," she said, after
scrutinizing every point. "For a wonder, it is
not typed. He seems to be very much in earnest. And his ideas about—her—remuneration
are certainly most liberal. Says nothing about
the mother—a cipher, probably. Girl too young
to be kept in Washington. I hope," she continued with sudden animation, "she is sound and
strong, and has had everything."

"Had everything, Mrs. Payne?"

"Measles and whooping-cough—and her first
love affair."

"I believe you will find my clients unexceptionable," said the principal, who was not fond of jesting upon serious subjects.

"But they really must send her photograph," Mrs. Payne exclaimed as she rose, eager to convey the result of her interview to Gwendolyn. "And I think you may safely write to Mr. Mordaunt that if everything goes well he may count upon Mrs. Spencer West."

"Mrs. Spencer West!" cried the principal, who, it will be recalled, was a reader of current prints. "Why, she is one of the most fashionable ladies in New York."

"Was. But her being so long in mourning has shut her in, and it is desired by her friends to rouse her from—ahem—her grief," went on Mrs. Payne nimbly. "We think she should have an object. You see, now, Mrs. Smith, how careful we should be to make no mistakes."

. "It is our aim to intermediate between only the most refined and cultivated principals," replied Mrs. Smith, with a high-toned sniff.

"And it is understood that the matter is *strictly* confidential."

"That, Madame, is the very foundation-stone of our enterprise."

"Good morning, then. Perhaps, not to lose time, you might write at once to Mr. Mordaunt."

Whatever the principal of the B. I. W. N. wrote, it brought a quick response. Mr. Mordaunt was much gratified by her efforts in his behalf, begged to inclose a photograph of his daughter, and would be in New York on Sunday for the purpose of settling preliminaries with Mrs. Spencer West.

"He is terribly business-like," said Gwendolyn, discontentedly. "But, dear me! the girl *is* pretty."

" 'Pretty' is tame," said Mrs. Payne, taking the picture from her friend. "She is beautiful, in a rather common way. Ugh! That frock cut half high, the hair done in a horn behind and stuck through with a dreadful ornamental pin! You should go to Paris, my dear, and put her in Pacquin's hands. But how very mature she looks for seventeen. She is like one of our girls in her third season."

"You can see 'local belle' written all over her. And those chains and rings and pins!" said fastidious Gwendolyn. "Oh! I could never do it in New York. And now to brace myself for that dreaded meeting with the fond papa!"

It was not written on the cards that the meeting in question should take place. Gwendolyn, through nervousness and a heavy cold combined, was in bed with a neuralgic headache when he came. She could hear from where she lay the clear, resonant tones, the masterful tread of the Senator, which seemed to fill up the spaces of her toy abode. She actually turned with her face to the wall, and stopped her ears with her fingers to avoid hearing more of him. Mrs. Payne scolded her afterward for her nonsense.

"I feel better satisfied, now I have seen him," said Kate. "There is something in him—I can't express it—that inspires confidence. He tells me the girl is motherless, and has been much indulged by her grandparents and relatives. He has been so busy with his affairs that he has seen comparatively little of her. She is affectionate and truthful, easy to lead, and hard to drive. She has never known anything but East Ephesus in her native State. She will come to you direct, and you ought to sail as early as you can.

Gwendolyn sat up in bed. Her headache was nearly gone. A desperate resolve to do the thing thoroughly, if at all, had come into her brain.

PART II

A few days later Mrs. West stood in the crowd on the platform at Jersey City awaiting a train from the West, and holding in her hand a hand-kerchief of azure silk, of which the duplicate was to be waved by her arriving charge. Her heart beat with an excitement it had not known for long.

She had not many moments of uncertainty. Even without the blue banner that bore down upon her in the hands of the prettiest creature in the throng, she would have recognized the original of the picture.

Miss Cecily Mordaunt, beaming with compla-cency, was attended by a man—gaunt, middle-aged, uncouth, with every sign of adoration of his companion written upon his countenance.

"You—you have got your maid?" asked Gwendolyn, peering about in search of that natural protector.

"Maid? Never had such a thing in my life," laughed Cecily. "And what would ha' been the use, when Mr. Lenvale would insist upon escort-ing me every step of the way. We stopped in

Chicago two hours, and took a hack and drove round to see the sights. I never was so surprised to see any one as Mr. Lenvale. He stole a march on the others, and sat in the smoking car, and came in to join me when East Ephesus was well out of sight. It almost seemed as if I had to have him, to carry all that truck.''

"That truck" was an assortment of faded flowers, bonbons, boxes, and baskets of fruit— with railway reading enough to stock a stall.

"They kept bringing it until the train moved off. Papa made me promise none of them should come along, but I couldn't help Mr. Lenvale, could I, now?''

"I have a carriage waiting on the other side of the ferry. We shall ask Mr. Lenvale to put your belongings into that, and then we shall not trouble him further," said Gwendolyn, in her soft, articulate voice. Poor Lenvale, although she smiled kindly, saw that his doom was sealed.

"He's a fright, isn't he?'' said heartless Cecily as they drove away uptown. "I'm really tired to death of him; but it wouldn't do exactly to let him know. When I saw you holding that blue handkerchief my heart was in my mouth with surprise. You look about as old as I am, or a very little older. 'Thank goodness she's young and pretty, and how well her clothes fit!' I said to Mr. Lenvale. When papa told me about you I cried for twenty-four hours without stopping, and all the girls came round to sympathize. I supposed you were a prim old party, with a whalebone back. Look here, now. Would you mind my kissing you?"

A week later they sailed for Genoa. Gwendolyn had engaged to attend them a courier-maid, certified against sea-sickness, and as possessing phenomenal accomplishments in the science of hotel bills and tips.

Senator Mordaunt, just then held in the vise of an important committee of inquiry over which he presided, had agreed to run over on a night train, breakfast with his daughter, see her off on the steamer, then hurry back to Washington. But at breakfast time arrived, instead of the Senator, a telegram, at sight of which Cecily first stamped her foot, then cried.

"I knew it! I have always had telegrams when I wanted my father most," she said between her sobs. "He can't get off, so sends me his blessing, and his compliments to you. Who wants to be blessed by telegraph?"

She was such a big, healthy, buoyant, fun-making being it was impossible to think of her as one who could suffer seriously or long, but Mrs. West saw that she loved her father, and that during a day or two of the voyage she lamented for him in silence.

It was rough off the coast, the skies dull, the company depressed. Gwendolyn lay most of this time in her berth, committing Cecily to the care of the courier-maid, and feeling too reckless of outer things even to read the letter from Washington marked "private and confidential" that had come aboard by special delivery as the ship was about to leave the dock. She had seen that it was from Mordaunt, and was full of injunctions about his daughter. It would keep.

On the afternoon of the third day out, the skies had cleared, sunshine fell warm and bright across the decks, there was a faint, sweet, far-away promise of spring in the light and steady breeze. The cabin passengers, to a man, woman, and child, felt its reviving influence. Creeping up on deck, Gwendolyn nestled into her chair, looked lazily across the rail, and bethought her of her letter.

After she had finished it she sat wondering. For the first time she realized the magnitude of her task. This was the cry of a strong man's heart for the right guidance and protection of his only child. Too late had come to him consciousness of the fact that Cecily had been left to environments that had done her mischief.

She had been on the verge of running away to marry a Mr. Parker Moffat, a crack baseball player, a young man encouraged by her silly, sentimental aunt.

The one worth talking about among her admirers—who made her the acknowledged sovereign of hearts in East Ephesus—had been flouted by her so successfully that it was hardly likely Angus McCrea would ever present himself to Mrs. West's notice. Should he do so, he was the sole representative of her 'home guard' whom Mordaunt would be willing for Cecily to receive Any overture from Moffat Mrs. West must incontinently quash.

And he is my "obliged and faithful J. Mordaunt," quoth Gwendolyn. "Well, I feel as if I had brought an explosive machine on board. I am afraid my charge is nothing more or less than an incorrigible flirt."

The rest of the voyage proved this indubitably. From the captain, who had her seated at table at his left hand, to the officers, great and petty, the deck stewards, the sailors with swabs, and the little cabin boys, every male thing belonging to the good ship was at Miss Mordaunt's beck and call.

The unmarried men among the passengers—including a missionary going out to Asia Minor, a German Baron, a magnate of Wall Street nursing a weak lung, a silk merchant from lower Broadway, two artists, and a popular young author—surrounded her chair, like a swarm of bees. The married men did the same whenever they were released from supervision by their wives; but it was a remarkably tranquil voyage, and the women were ordinarily all on deck.

Gwendolyn's sense of propriety suffered under such fierce publicity. Miss Mordaunt's sayings and doings were bandied everywhere. The people aboard who were previously known to Mrs. West set afloat the story that her comet was a cousin or niece going to join her family. Most of these good folk thought it would be a happy day for Mrs. West when she could surrender her charge and fold her hands in repose.

Vigilance—perpetual vigilance—was evidently to be the price of Gwendolyn's peace. The overwhelming spirits, the reckless sayings, the audacious doings of Cecily began at breakfast time and ended not till Gwendolyn forced her to go below at bedtime. And the distressing part of it was that the chaperon found herself, too, laughing at the girl's nonsense—giggling helplessly, irrepressibly. Cecily affected her like champagne or St. Moritz air.

At Gibraltar Miss Mordaunt said she was

going to cable to her papa. When they were off again in the Mediterranean she threw her arms around Gwendolyn's neck and admitted that she had cabled to some one else besides papa. No coaxings could induce her to say more than this, and Gwendolyn felt uncomfortable. At Genoa the girl received two cable messages, sent in care of the captain of the ship, who delivered them to her with massive gallantry.

From that moment it seemed that Cecily's spirit of mischief had broken loose worse than before. Mrs. West and the courier-maid, both of them secretly devoted to her, were kept forever on the alert to watch her vagaries. Upon the tourist track of Europe she left behind her a corruscating trail of anecdotes.

As the summer progressed Gwendolyn resigned herself to being a marked woman, as the guardian of the most original young person who had appeared in the best-known haunts in a generation. It was marvelous to see how Cecily's slang, loud speaking and dressing, and petty offenses against good breeding had dropped away from her. The outer shell of her became conventional, but that was all.

* * *

When the handsome and well-born Marquis de San Miniato followed them to Luzerne, and asked

Mrs. West for the hand of her charming charge in marriage, Gwendolyn felt herself pulled up as with too hard a curb.

"Of course you will not consider him," she said, much more confused than was the heroine of the hour.

"I *was* thinking a little of getting married in Italy in the fall," answered Miss Mordaunt, pensively. "A wedding would be so sweet in that lovely old Duomo at Florence. And I couldn't have it in the Duomo unless I married a Catholic, I suppose."

"Cecily!"

"Gwen, dear, you can't do it. You haven't the cut of a chaperon's jib. Why, San Miniato took us first for a pair of schoolgirls, and Mimms for our governess. You're a failure, and I'm a terror; but we *have* had a good time, haven't we?"

"Cecily, your father—I have an idea he would dislike this more than anything you could do. Don't, don't answer Miniato now. Let me tell him to go to America and see your papa. That is the only decent thing to do."

"The others—all but one—asked *me* first," said Cecily, dimpling. "But it's a shame to tease you, poor, dear little soul. Send Miniato packing, if you like. I don't generally—right away. I keep them on as friends, like poor Mr. Lenvale, till I can't stand them a minute longer. Anyhow, old Miniato's a goose to think I'd marry out of my own country and live away from papa."

Gwendolyn had the tact to say nothing. In a moment Cecily began again.

"You've been so awfully good to me, Gwenny. If I had had a mother, I'd have wanted her to be like you. But my mother died when I was born, and I had no one but an aunt and grandmother, who—papa, couldn't get along with them, and I don't blame him. He has been awfully gener-ous—but kept away. You know he has made money himself, but he inherited a lot from his mother's brother on condition he'd change his name. The Mordaunts were an older family than the Atwells, and my uncle didn't want them to die out—"

"Atwell! It can't be possible!" cried Gwen-dolyn, "John Rufus Atwell?"

"Yes, that was his full name. Did you ever know him?"

"Once, long ago," said Gwendolyn, in a maze of astonishment.

"I want to tell you a secret—if you won't ask me a single question in return," went on the girl, filled with her own affairs. "Although not to San Miniato, I am really going to be married. I've left my heart, my real heart, at home, with the best fellow in the world. When I got to Gibraltar I kept a promise I'd made to him, and cabled out that he might come to us in September. By the time we get to Paris he'll be there, and then, Gwenny, then—oh! You'll be a jolly, easy-going chaperon, and I the happiest girl in the world. Now I'm off to take Mimms for a perfectly horrid little walk, to see Thorwaldsen's Lion. If I ever get home to blessed East Ephesus I'll walk out by myself after dark, see if I don't."

Gwendolyn's face, when she was left alone with these surprising revelations, was very pale. After deliberation she took out a cable code Mr. Mordaunt had sent her for exigencies, and patched together words conveying the following message:

"Fear daughter's intention to marry. Had better come at once. Meet us Paris. Will watch faithfully till then."

* * * * *

They had found refuge from observation in a quiet and cozy little hotel just out of the Champs Élysées. For some days following their arrival in Paris Cecily had been under a spell of gentleness. She did not again allude to her hopes and prospects, and Gwendolyn, trusting the matter had blown by, said nothing, but never left her side. Cecily did not know that her father was expected. It had been agreed between Mordaunt and his daughter's chaperon to give his visit the air of a happy afterthought.

When the day came that should bring relief to the citadel Gwendolyn breathed a long sigh. Soon after their early breakfast Cecily asked for the company of Mimms to make some purchases at the Bon Marché. She had equipped herself so charmingly, her face and person breathed such radiancy of good health and happiness, that Gwendolyn could not resist giving the child a parting squeeze and kiss.

"I shall wait for you to go in to the second breakfast, dear," she said, affectionately.

"Ah, Gwen, how I love you!" cried the girl with a sudden burst. "Never be angry with me; I was not brought up like other girls."

She was gone. The little open cab containing her and the grim Miss Mimms rattled down the stony street to the Elysian Fields. Gwendolyn sighed.

"She has tangled herself in my heart-strings, certainly. I could not bear her to think me treacherous. But my first duty was to *him.*"

As the hours passed she grew fidgety, rearranged the ornaments, the flowers, the books, in their pretty salon—ran to the window to look at many cabs, and when at last the one arrived that contained John Mordaunt, was quite unaware of it.

He was treading on the heels of the garçon who came up to announce him—in her presence before she realized it.

"I knew you long ago through Mrs. Payne; but you could not be supposed to identify me," he said, with strong feeling, as he took her hand. "You have not changed in the least. And to think that all these years I could not find out whom you had married."

Gwendolyn blushed deeply, and drew her hand from his.

"It was so good of you to relieve my anxiety about our girl," she answered. "Now I begin to think she said it to frighten me."

"No matter, since I am here. But where is she—my darling torment?"

Gwendolyn explained.

"Then sit down and let us learn each other all over again," said this taking-for-granted Senator.

Gwendolyn did not know why she obeyed; the moments flew, she telling, he listening, and vice versa. They were rudely interrupted by the bursting open of the door and the entrance of Miss Mimms, aghast.

"Oh! sir! Oh! m'm," she cried, breathless. "I've lost her. For the last hour I've been sitting in the waiting-room at the Bon Marché, as she bid me, and she's never come back. And at last a little boy came and put this note in my hand for Mrs. West, and told me the young lady said I was to go along home to the hotel."

"My own Gwenny, forgive me," ran the note. "I couldn't bear to meet him in a horrid, ordinary way. We are off on top a tram to take our luncheon at Versailles, and by five o'clock I'll be back and introduce him to you in proper fashion."

"If it's that scoundrel Moffat, he'll never bring her back," shouted John Mordaunt. "He well knows she has a fortune from her uncle coming to her on her marriage with no matter whom. He'll get her off somewhere and manage to have a ceremony performed before he is interrupted. He—"

"I believe in Cecily," said Gwendolyn, quietly. "Let us, you and I, Mr. Mordaunt, go directly in pursuit of them. Cecily is foolish, reckless, but she would never give you—and me—that pain."

"Then it is you who have made her know herself! God bless you," said the agitated man. "Ah! Gwendolyn, why did I not have you from the first?"

313

* * * * *

Miss Mimms afterward averred that you might have knocked her down with a feather when, that afternoon, the whole party of four came driving up to the door of the hotel. (Miss M. had spent most of her day suspended like a banner for royalty out of the windows of the first floor.) He, the young lady's papa—looking like a general or a judge, she couldn't exactly say which, but as fine a show of a man as she wished ever to see; Mrs. West, so happy and smiling, just like a little girl that has got a present she'd been crying for; and Miss Mordaunt—well, nobody could beat her for looks and pretty ways. At the very top of the steps didn't she seize Mimms and hug her, and introduce her to "Mr. Angus McCrea, the young man that ran away with me this morning, and that's going to be my husband"?

For Mr. Angus McCrea it was who had wooed Cecily's roving heart into his safe-keeping—a fine, manly young fellow, to whom even John Mordaunt, the discourager of sons-in-law, could not take exception.

"And at any rate," whispered saucy Cecily, "it's easy to see they were old sweethearts, Gwen and papa. They are so taken up with each other, Angus, you and I might give them a lesson in self-control."

www.ingramcontent.com/pod-product-compliance
Lightning Source LLC
Chambersburg PA
CBHW020947030726
47496CB00005B/1385